PRAISE

C000005398

"E. Rachael Hard
we make and the u̶̶̶̶
sometimes occur. But, what if we had a second chance,
even after we died? What would we do differently?
Would we more carefully make choices, knowing that
our choices have consequences for others?

E. Rachael Hardcastle expertly explores the choices
that we make, the unintended consequences for others,
and the hope of redemption!"

Paul Reeves, Impact Radio USA

"Noah Finn and the Art of Suicide will challenge
your views on mortality, religion, ethics and many
more, set against a backdrop that without skilful
authorship could have moved focus away from the
story. To use as a background a world event that
continues to shock us many years on and being able to
maintain the reader's focus on the story, with its
interesting characters rather than that world event per
se, shows a maturity and writing ability that really
impressed me. The ability to make people think and
rethink strongly held principles is what separates a
good storyteller from a professional author. This book,
with its open structure that moves along at a good
pace, does just that."

Malcolm Clarke, Durham County Councillor

"In this novella Rachael is grappling with such
philosophical issues of purpose, relationships, afterlife,
faith, religion. In fact, the meaning of life and death.
She does this in a very creative way for her
readership."

Emma Truelove, Radio Royal

Also By E. Rachael Hardcastle

Finding Pandora

World
Heaven
Infinity
Eternity
The Complete Collection

Aeon Infinitum

Run For Your Life

Other Titles

Forgotten Faith
Noah Finn & the Art of Suicide

NOAH FINN & THE ART OF SUICIDE

A NOVELLA

☠

E. RACHAEL HARDCASTLE

First printed in 2017.

ISBN-13: 978-1-9999688-1-6

Curious Cat Books
West Yorkshire, UK
www.erachaelhardcastle.com

PROLOGUE

☠

Death is not the end.

That's what I'm hoping to teach this 28-year-old exhausted janitor, Noah Finn, before it's too late.

It's my duty.

I've been watching Noah since the day he was born. I witnessed his first breath, cheered him on when he braved that first wobbly step, then the next. I've laughed at every birthday party. I even danced at his wedding.

In fact, for every second of every minute of every hour of every day of Noah's rather short but beautifully meaningful life, I've been there.

Naturally, I was also in the room for the birth of his fraternal twin sister, Annaliese, and until yesterday morning I was watching over her, too.

But watching isn't all I do; isn't all I'm capable of, known for, *hated* for. It is, however, easily the most rewarding part of my job. Observation is merely the first and kindest step on their road to a tailored afterlife.

For I am Death.

I will take you when you can take no more, end your suffering and numb your pain, even when you deserve to feel it all.

Then I'll exchange one wasted life for another, just like Noah's.

Especially Noah's.

Because a person, sometimes *people,* have to die for anyone (*everyone*) to live. It's the unwritten law; a rule I cannot change and joyfully enforce.

To most it seems unfair, but it never discriminates, proving Death is not the end.

Never is.

Never has been.

Never will be.

LESSON ONE
DENIAL

☠

E. Rachael Hardcastle

Chapter One
THE STATION

☠

September 11th 2001

Startled by the roaring of a passing train, Noah Finn awakens in a bustling subway station.

He's stretched across an uncomfortable metal bench. His throat is dry. His limbs tremble in fear, but of what he isn't sure.

It's 08:46 am.
Noah is going to be late for work again.

Disturbed by an unusual nightmare, Noah misses the announcement and drowns out a panicked conversation between two businessmen somewhere in his peripheral vision.

Despite hating his job as a janitor, Noah scrambles to his feet as not to be late.

He jogs to the edge of the platform and the doors slide open. Commuters surround him; all of them faceless ghouls through his exhaustion, and Noah curses before fighting through their sweating bodies.

In the calm of a now empty carriage, dirty and damaged as a result of discarded litter and anti-social behavior over the years, he sits in a silver seat just seconds before a middle-aged, husky policeman bounds down the aisle.

The doors close and the train jolts forward.

It picks up speed and disappears into the eerie tunnel. Noah squints beneath the dim yellow carriage lights and attempts to read a newspaper.

They flicker and temporarily go out. Noah slams the paper down in frustration.

When they come back on he's not alone.

Christopher Saint is a heavy-set man, over six feet tall, with milk chocolate skin and warm hazel eyes; the complete opposite of Noah Finn who is a blond, blue-eyed ghostly silhouette. Not at all athletic as many of his past girlfriends - always considerate of his feelings - had pointed out.

They sit beside one another in silence, both staring at the ground.

Against the man's frame, Noah feels consumed and meek, the way he always felt under the watchful eye of his father; an ant beneath the magnifying glass.

He's about to clear his throat and say 'excuse me' to sit elsewhere when Christopher turns to him.

"What you in for?" he asks.

"Work," Noah grumbles. "You?"

"Same. Rather the subway than a cab. I *hate* cabs. Maniac drivers, endless queues of traffic." He pauses. "Got hit by one 'bout two years back, y'know."

Noah sniffs, turns away and pretends to read the newspaper.

Perhaps taking the subway was a mistake.

Actually, he prefers cabs. As an ex-public transport employee, Noah remembers removing gum from beneath otherwise tidy seats, mopping up urine from drunken party-goers and being spat on by graffiti artists he'd challenged. In the past, New York City had been unkind to shift workers like Noah. His tolerance of chatty strangers back then had soon worn thin, so he quit.

After his uncle, a highly respected banker like his father, Rodger, had put in a good word for him, desperately trying to pull his cocaine-addicted nephew from poverty, Noah took the job mopping floors and polishing windows. A job offered through pity.

Yet another mistake.

And still a massive failure.

"Name's Christopher Saint," says the man, extending a rough hand.

Hesitant, Noah lifts his head to acknowledge the greeting but he ignores the outstretched palm.

Christopher gestures at the beads of sweat lingering on Noah's brow.

"Hot in here?"

Noah startles and wipes it away with the back of his hand. His temperature's fine but Christopher's right, he's sweating a little.

He reaches for his navy handkerchief, usually folded neatly in his top pocket, but today it's missing.

He checks his pants. Nothing there either.

Noah begins a frantic search of the carriage.

"It's hot for most people at first," Christopher says, picking imaginary dirt from his nails. "Here, use mine."

Noah offers half a smile and reluctantly takes the handkerchief, still scanning the floor.

Engraved with his father's initials, Noah gave it to his sister as a memorable 'something blue' on her wedding day. He even used it at work once to wipe some smeared fingerprints from his boss's office window.

Ever since, he's gone nowhere without it.

It reminds him how worthless he is in comparison.

16

from his upper lip and chin.

"How do you know my name? How did you get here so fast?"

Noah searches the tiny cabin for a weapon.

Light-headed and frightened, he grabs an empty soda bottle from an over-flowing bin and slaps it forcefully against his palm. He fully intends to thwack Christopher's skull if he creeps any closer, but makes the mistake of looking down at the label first.

December 24th 1988

Noah is fifteen years old in the back seat of his father's Ford, bashing an empty bottle he found against his sister's head.

"Noah, cut it out!"

He laughs; taunts her a little more.

Christmas or no Christmas, Noah doesn't want to visit his grandfather in Chelsea. Despite the house being bigger and grander than theirs, on a good day it smells of mothballs and ointment. On a not-so-good day, the air is bitter with urine.

His parents, Rodger and Laura, always take Noah and Annaliese to visit relatives during the holidays, leaving them less time to play with their friends.

"Why do we have to go see Grandpa?"

"Because he's alone and he's elderly and because I say so," says his mother.

"I like going to see Grandpa." Annaliese scolds him, knocking the soda bottle into the footwell. "He tells some good stories, you just don't listen."

Noah sulks. "He never did any of the things in them, though. It's all just bullshit, right, Dad?"

His father glances at him in the rearview mirror and shakes his head, but, trying to concentrate on the road, says nothing.

"You watch your language! We've discussed this," his mother begins. "Grandpa has Dementia. Sometimes he gets confused but he means well. He bought you gifts this year so when you see him, remember your manners."

Noah folds his arms. "Why do we always have to do what *you* want? I could be spending Christmas with my friends."

Annaliese scowls. "*I like Grandpa!* He's family, Noah!"

"*He's family,*" he mocks. "But it's boring!"

In the mirror, his father's eyes narrow. His lips scrunch together like he's sucking a lemon drop.

"I don't want to hear it," says his mother. "One day when you're old you'll appreciate a visit, too."

"Oh, whatever-"

Noah's father reaches round and swats at him,

narrowly missing his scrawny shins as they drum against the back of his seat.

"Now you listen to me-"

"RODGER WATCH OUT!"

The car swerves.

His mother screams.

☠

September 11th 2001

"Oh good, you're back! How can two siblings born on the same day to be so *different*? Oh well! How do you feel about the word *denial*?"

Still frozen by the memory, it takes Noah a few seconds to regain his confidence. Then, using the bottle, he pounds the seat a couple more times for effect.

"Just back off and tell me who you are!"

Christopher nods as if to confirm his suspicion. "Ignorance and denial, among other crimes. Selfishness, hastiness, a judgmental and negative attitude. These stand out the most, I think."

"I *beg* your pardon?"

"Oh, save your anger, Mr. Finn, there's more where that came from. Surely I'm not the first to point out how untrusting and ungrateful you are? Not to mention impatient and, to be honest, your timekeeping is *atrocious*."

He taps his watch and waits for an argumentative response, but doesn't get one.

"We're going to have to do this the hard way, I can tell."

Without warning, Christopher charges forward and wrestles the bottle away, prising it from Noah's fingers with his rough hands.

Noah panics and dodges his grip, then sets off running. He locates an escape route through to the next carriage at the far end. Inbuilt on the other side could be the emergency brake, and if Noah can reach it before Christopher apprehends him, he'll be one step closer to an explanation, to the authorities, and to being late, *again*, for work.

I can make it. I can make it. Don't look back.

Christopher can only laugh. Runners and escape artists are common in his line of work.

His tongue slides playfully between his teeth as he aims with one eye closed, then sends the bottle spinning through the air. It bops Noah on the back of the head.

He turns and catches his foot on a chair leg; hits the floor like a sack of potatoes.

When he opens his eyes, he feels no pain.

He's in paradise.

Chapter Four
THE WEDDING

☠

October 6th 2000

Noah is standing beside his twin sister, Annaliese, at the back of St Paul's Chapel on her wedding day.

Their arms are linked on one side; on the other she's holding a bouquet of pink and white roses, intermingled with tiny white daisies and flourishing lilies to match those plaited through her golden hair. Her silk dress is antique white with a crochet neckline and lace up back.

Noah only understands what all this means from listening to her obsessive wedding plans while he and his soon-to-be brother-in-law, Jose Aberlado, drank beer on Annaliese's balcony.

A balcony once belonging to their grandfather.

Noah thinks Annaliese looks beautiful but

anxious; she's masked her fear well with make-up. There are two thin streaks where she's been crying, which Noah isn't sure is entirely with happiness.

"Here, take this, y'know, for luck," he says, before rolling up his handkerchief and sticking it in the top her bouquet.

She giggles, then holds her head higher.

Noah is doing his utmost to hold it together himself. Despite there being only four minutes between them, she'll always be his little sister, and today he's giving her away to a man who loves Annaliese almost as much as he does.

Almost.

Andrea Bocelli's *The Prayer* begins to play over the speakers.

Aunts and uncles, cousins, friends and colleagues are celebrating their love for his sister.

Love she more than deserves.

Over the years she's been there for Noah; rooted beside him through the loss of their parents, even at such a young age, then providing a stable place to lay his head during his agonizing divorce, right up until his more recent successful drugs rehabilitation.

Everything I am today, I am because of Annaliese.

Noah finds three empty seats on the front row.

His chest tightens.

On two of those seats are delicate red roses to represent their missing parents. The third is for Noah when his role in the wedding is over and he can finally relax.

In the car, Annaliese admitted to hoping their parents were watching from Heaven.

Noah agreed and added, 'if there *is* a Heaven'.

Obviously, he's now regretting that.

They're about half way down the aisle without incident when he glances at Annaliese and gives her arm a reassuring pat.

The hard part is nearly over.

He turns his attention back to his seat but it's no longer empty. Silently clapping, not quite in slow motion, is Christopher Saint.

Noah stops dead. So does the music.

His sister walks ahead as if accompanied by his ghost. The ceremony continues regardless.

At the altar she even kisses imaginary Noah's cheek, hands her flowers – and her something blue - to the Maid of Honor, and takes Jose's hand.

All the while Noah is watching from the aisle.

Nobody does or says a thing until Christopher beckons him forward.

He narrows his eyes and lets out a rage-fuelled

roar.

"WHAT THE HELL IS GOING ON HERE?"

The room begins to spin, then fades away.

When Noah opens his eyes, he's back in the carriage.

Chapter Five
THE INCLINE

☠

September 11th 2001

Christopher aids Noah to a stance. His head and hips aren't bruised; aren't painful at all, in fact.

Shaken, Noah whispers, "What *was* that?"

He dusts down his clothing. His hands are shaking. He's chewing his bottom lip, fighting tears.

"It felt so *real*."

"Just a memory, I'm afraid."

"Can we go back?"

"*We?*"

"Well, it *was* you on the front row, wasn't it?"

"Yes."

"And you took me there; brought me back?"

After a sharp inhalation, Christopher says, "I did."

"Then let's go!"

"No," says Christopher.

"What do you mean *no*? Why not?"

"I could see you'd be a difficult case. I thought I could ease you into your first lesson with something pleasant and familiar. I was wrong."

Noah's brow furrows. "A lesson?"

"Yes, your first lesson."

"To teach me *what*, exactly?"

"That you're dead," says Christopher matter-of-factly.

"I know I'm dead."

"You do *now*."

"I did before!" he argues.

"Before this you were dreaming, apparently."

Christopher pauses then heads back to his original seat in the carriage. Noah trails behind and taps him on the shoulder.

"So will you?"

"Will I what?"

"Take me to see Annaliese!"

Christopher clears his throat. "Oh, no, sorry."

"WHY NOT?"

"I wasn't really supposed to do it the first time. Shock therapy is against the rules. Effective most of the time, though. *Most of the time.*"

Noah slumps in the seat beside him. "*Damn you!*"

"Oh, I wouldn't say things like that down

here."

"Hang on, not only am I dead but I'm in *Hell* too? I'm by no means perfect, but-"

Christopher grins. "This is going to be fun, I can tell. Look, Mr. Finn, I like you, but you should relax. There's a long way to go before *that* decision gets made."

"What decision?"

"The 'moving on' decision. So, put your feet up for a while."

"That officer won't like that," Noah says.

"I think we've established there is no officer."

Noah folds his arms. "Anyone ever tell you how exasperating you are?"

"Only every day." Christopher smiles.

He fishes in his pocket for the handkerchief and hands it back to Noah, gesturing he take it without further questions.

It's not his own, but it'll do.

They sit in silence for a while, swaying with the movement of the train and listening to the expected clack-clacking.

"Do you know who I am, Mr. Finn?"

Noah folds the handkerchief to stall.

After a few seconds, he replies, "You're God."

Christopher snorts and begins to laugh until he notices Noah's blank expression.

"You're close."

"You sound pretty God-like to me. If not Him, who are you?"

"I am Death," Christopher says, adding a crooked smile to ease (or so he hopes) the tension. "I adopted this friendlier name, appearance, and accent for the purpose of our journey. I'm a watcher and protector of travelers, do you get it?"

"Very funny," Noah says and rolls his eyes. "What do your other clients think of your sense of humor?"

"'Other clients'?"

"The people you kill and verbally abuse on this godforsaken train."

"*Ouch.* You know, Mr. Finn, you're getting ahead of yourself. Bitterness is lesson three. Still, in the interest of progression, of the two thousand nine hundred and ninety-five - wait, make that six – I'm counseling now, you're the first to stick up your nose."

"There's nobody else here." Noah checks over his shoulder to be sure. "I don't understand *any* of this."

"Allow me time to explain and you will. What do you have left, Mr. Finn, if not time?" Christopher waits for a bite that never comes. "Humor me? I'd like to get to know you better."

Noah uncrosses his arms. "From all the horrible things you said earlier, I think you know

36

me pretty well. Besides, you're Death and I'm dead. You're in the life-taking business and I committed suicide - you *could* say I made your job easy. That's all there is to know."

Christopher wrings his hands together. "First of all, you did not commit suicide. You wouldn't be here if you did. Secondly, I don't initiate the end of a life, I simply deal with the aftermath."

Noah has nothing else to say on the matter and frankly, neither does Christopher.

"Feel that?"

Noah scowls, says nothing.

"We're on an *incline*," Christopher says. "Are you going to co-operate or should I ask the driver to put this thing in reverse?"

He pauses until Noah's expression changes, finally understanding the insinuation.

"Good boy," he says, "Now, where was I? Ah yes! Lesson number one... denial."

Chapter Six
PUSH COMES TO SHOVE

☠

Christopher Saint takes Noah's hand and leads him to the train's automated doors.

The carriage is still in motion.

Noah tenses. "I'm not ready."

"Sure you are, it'll be easy. What's the last thing you remember before the station?"

"Nothing, nothing at all."

Christopher sighs. "Don't be afraid of me. I'm not going to hurt you, Mr. Finn. I can't. You're dead."

Noah relaxes, feeling silly. "You've been watching me since the platform?"

"Oh, *long* before then. I'm an observer. So should you be, then you'd know where I'm going with this."

Christopher hits the emergency brake, prises open the doors and gives Noah a shove.

Suddenly he's struggling against a vicious

wind, shuddering as his hair is ruffled. He can hear the flap flap of his overalls as they patter against his chest.

He's not feeling well. His lungs are tight.

He's anxious. No, *terrified*.

His heart begins to thump. Occasionally it skips a beat, dances a little.

Adrenaline courses through Noah's veins, sending emergency messages to his senses and they launch into overdrive.

In the distance Noah hears the whirring of a turbine engine. The usual honking of traffic is especially loud today. The emergency services are busy, too.

His fingers are vibrating through the rail he's holding. So are the building's foundations.

He panics and opens his eyes, releasing the memory.

Christopher grabs his overalls and hauls him inside the carriage.

Noah is pleased to feel oxygen filling his lungs, even if it's still an illusion. He waits a moment to make sure his chest is expanding, realizing he's safe.

"You *pushed* me!"

"No, I *prompted* you."

Noah backs away. "How am I supposed to trust you now?"

"You're not. We're not friends, Mr. Finn. I'm just here to do a job. You're here to learn the lesson and I'm the only teacher available. Your options are limited."

"But why did you push me?"

"Because you wouldn't have jumped had I not," he replies. "This time, however, you might just."

Noah snorts and shakes his head. "Who in their right mind would throw themselves off a moving train *voluntarily*?"

Christopher returns to his uncomfortable silver seat.

"How about the man who almost threw himself off a high-rise office building?"

Almost.

Noah falls quiet.

The automated doors slink shut, indicating he should probably sit too, but after a few minutes of staring at his shoes, Noah looks up and in a low, calm voice, says, "I didn't kill myself, did I?"

Christopher shakes his head. "You were doing a fine job of pretending. Stepped over the railing and *everything*. I was tempted to give you a nudge to be honest."

"I thought you said you didn't meddle in the circumstances."

"I don't, so I didn't. *I'm* not the one who never finishes what he starts, though. Are you

41

frightened of missing something, like the world really *needs* you? Hardly! Adultery. Divorce. Drugs. Not to mention you were raised by a criminal and abandoned by your twin just last year."

"Uncle Joe got me a job, I'm grateful."

"Are you? You hated your job, yet you still did it. Why? Because your father worked there, or because like your uncle, you planned to steal hundreds of thousands of dollars when the opportunity arose?"

"No, I just wanted to pay my bills," he says, "and Annaliese didn't abandon me, nor did my parents. They died in a car accident!"

Christopher waves it off. "Same thing. Someone, somewhere, will be blaming *you* for leaving the party early. My case is strong, you *are* a selfish, hasty fool with no regard for other people's feelings or sacrifices. Yet, the universe still tried to save you. Did its damn best, too. You just couldn't take the hint. "

The lines on Noah's forehead tighten.

"Correct me if I'm wrong," Christopher continues, "but you've considered suicide before. Something stopped you then, too. What was it the last time?" He scratches his chin for effect. "That mutt on the bridge. It ran in your path, made you swerve back on the road."

"It would have been unreasonable of me to

42

take a life worth living," Noah grumbles.

"Your life *was* worth living. The dog, however, was severely injured and died the next day anyway." Christopher shrugs. "That animal saved your life, Mr. Finn."

Noah remembers flooring the gas; his bare hands tight around the leather steering wheel and his drug-fuelled eyes focused on the bridge's already damaged barrier.

He drove over the curb to greet it.

But a limping Collie appeared suddenly in his headlights, heading in the opposite direction. Its panic-stricken eyes caused Noah to slam on his brakes.

He yanked the wheel.

The car skidded in a semi-circle.

Finally, he came to a diagonal halt in the middle of the road. The angry driver behind gave him the finger, then sped off into the distance.

"Am I losing you?" Christopher asks.

Noah catches his breath.

"Wh-what do you want me to say? Should I apologize; be thankful? Isn't that just the way the world works? Someone dies for another to live?"

"You don't know the *half* of it. But no, I just want you to admit you're afraid of me."

"Something I never denied."

"I disagree," Christopher explains. "Each time you've attempted to take your own life, you've been struggling with the very basics of adulthood. Finances: the rope snapped. Family: the dog made you swerve. Grief: the plane finally stole your thunder. The universe intervened every time, you just never took the hint. You've caused too many problems; interfered with the natural order of things. Something, somewhere, decided you're no longer worth the effort."

Noah groans and sinks lower in his seat.

"The first lesson is always denial, Mr. Finn. To accept you're dead and the reason - or reasons - takes the most time. You're human. Somewhere in that immature, easily influenced little brain is - besides curiosity and ego - a natural survival instinct. You may not have wanted to live in the past, but you most *certainly* did not want to die. You were afraid. So why did you waste so much time plotting various, ultimately pointless escape routes? As you can see, death isn't the end and if you let it, emotion can torment you even now.

"Know what I find so interesting about *your* circumstances, Mr. Finn? Your death - although forced upon you - was a kind, quick, ideally timed escape route. I've met thousands of others today, none of whom were so lucky. You ought to be thankful, but you're not. Evidence to support my accusations of selfishness, ungratefulness and guilt. You *finally* got what you wanted - maybe what you deserved - and you're still unhappy. Now come with me," he says, "there's something I want to show you."

E. Rachael Hardcastle

Chapter Seven
AMERICAN AIRLINES

☠

American Airlines Flight 11 crashes into floors ninety-three through ninety-nine of the World Trade Center's north tower. It kills everyone on board the plane and hundreds of innocent people working inside the building.

Noah feels Christopher's hard shove against his shoulders.

The metal bars go first. Then he's tumbling, disappearing into a thick, hot smog at high speed.

Falling.

Falling.

Though Christopher is nowhere around, Noah feels his guidance. What he's about to witness, Death wants ingrained in his memory for eternity.

Shock renders the past Noah unconscious.

He feels nothing. Not the wind in his face nor his burning skin. He's oblivious to the cries for help and passes them in seconds anyway.

The present Noah wants to rewind the scene to

help those people; to know more about the passengers on the plane, the circumstances, to find and evacuate his colleagues, to warn everybody.

Some of those office workers were difficult to tolerate but none deserved to die like that, or at all.

When the smoke clears, Noah's final sights are of an unrecognizable rooftop.

The vision ends.

Christopher pulls him back.

Through the lingering memory, Noah smacks his clothing to put out invisible flames. He sinks to his feet; hides behind the closest seat.

He screams.

He cries.

He rocks.

"All those innocent people!"

Christopher nods. "It's very tragic."

"But *why?*"

"Why what? Why did you have to die painlessly instead of them? You tell me. Why did the terrorists on that plane do what they did? I'd say on faith." He pauses. "What you *really* want to know, Mr. Finn, is why does *anyone* do *anything?*"

He sniffs. "Is that a rhetorical question?"

"By all means answer if you can."

"I can't. Is it something to do with the meaning of life?"

"Pfft! If you ever figure *that* one out, you let me know."

Noah wipes his eyes and nose on his sleeve.

"Don't you ask people questions before agreeing to take them to the afterlife? Can you refuse; return them?"

Christopher offers half a smile. "You can't go back, Mr. Finn. You're dead."

"Not me, *them*. Those innocent people. They wanted to live and I didn't. This is backward!"

Christopher squats beside him. "Sometimes I'd like to. Others I wish I'd killed myself – like you. I mean, I knew you were heading my way and you were so exhausting to keep alive! After a while the universe just gave up. It happens sometimes. People can be cruel; today I think humanity proved my point. And so did you."

"But what about God? Can He fix all this?"

"If by 'all this' you mean today's terrible tragedy, then no." He pauses. "If I told you there is no God, what would you say?"

"I'd believe you because God – *any* God - wouldn't let this happen."

"The God you know wouldn't, but how well do you actually know Him? If you could ask and He told you it *was* all His fault, you'd label Him evil, perhaps no longer worship Him, right?"

49

Noah nods. "Maybe, I guess. Is that wrong?"

"It's not *right*."

"You'll have to elaborate," says Noah, confused.

Christopher settles beside Noah on the floor and places a palm on his knee to stop it juddering. Like many of his clients, Christopher can see he's fighting guilt and fear.

Why was he spared pain if others must suffer?

"It is *I* who follows you through life, Mr. Finn. I judge you, laugh with you, laugh *at* you, cringe at your mistakes and celebrate when you correct them. I hear your prayers and curses. *I* am the one and only entity, not God," he explains.

For a few minutes Noah rocks in quiet contemplation. Christopher gives him chance to process the news; let it sink in a bit.

Then Noah has an epiphany. Excited, he jumps to his feet.

"Then *you're* God."

Face in his hands, Christopher grumbles, "There is no God. There is only me and the universe I exist in."

"But you just said-"

Christopher halts him. "'God' is the term humans have attached to the parts of me they like."

"And the parts they dislike, including this conversation?" Noah asks, looking down on the entity in which he once believed.

Christopher grins. "I see you're still capable of sarcasm. When it's something they dislike, then I am Death. Some call me Divorce, Depression, Sickness, Tedious Conversations. I could go on."

Noah turns his back on Christopher as he chews his fingernails.

All this time I've been worshipping Death*? If Christopher Saint is the one true entity - birth, death and all in between - is he responsible for humanity's suffering, for* my *suffering?*

Worried, Christopher reaches out and touches Noah on the shoulder. As expected, he flinches.

"I can't hurt you, Mr. Finn, and I don't want to. I observe the Earth; I have no influence, at least not anymore."

"The religions of the world seem to think you do. Are they *all* wrong?"

Noah shakes his head, realizing he's unlikely to get anything further on the matter. He gestures at Christopher's appearance.

"And what relevance is this? Why a tall black guy?"

"Your human mind isn't capable of accepting my true form, so I took another's. His name was Ogugbuaja Lauren. Born in America but of Nigerian origin on his father's side. An elementary school teacher in Brooklyn. His friends called him Oggie."

"*Called.* So he's dead. You knew him well?"

"I know everyone well."

"And what did he do to deserve this honor?"

"He died," Christopher says, "for you."

LESSON TWO
GUILT

Chapter Eight
HIS NAME WAS OGGIE

☠

From his pants pocket, Christopher produces a photograph of himself, a man named Ogugbuaja Lauren. He's standing at the back of an elementary school class, smiling proudly and approximately two feet higher than most of the others.

He doesn't care. Despite his size the children love him. He loves them, too, in his own way.

Prior to that photograph the children were learning about religion, something Oggie had never really invested in, but understood and respected. Members of his family were religious, as were some of his friends. He wanted the children to care for one another despite having different beliefs; build their relationships on trust and personality, heart and soul, rather than a label.

He was doing a wonderful job, too.

"Oggie was a great guy," Christopher tells Noah. "All he wanted was to help people; gave blood, volunteered at fundraisers, hospitals, rehabilitation centers. He had no family, though. Get where I'm going with this?"

Noah's hands begin to tremble. He puts them up against the doors. For a second he wishes they would open and suck him out.

"If I'm a murderer, we should put this train in reverse."

"He *did* die saving your life, Mr. Finn, but don't worry, it evens out eventually. Since birth the universe was preparing him as a sacrifice, but *you* didn't really kill him, someone else did."

"Yet I'm still responsible, like manslaughter?"

"Well someone died for him once, too, so manslaughter isn't the word either. In case you hadn't figured it out yet, you died for someone as well – everyone does."

Noah pauses. "*I* died for someone?"

"We'll get to it soon," says Christopher, dismissing Noah's concerns with a wave of his hand. "Are you ready for your second lesson?"

"I passed the first?"

He grins. "You've accepted you're dead, right?"

Noah is surprised. So far he's been failing everything thrown at him, or so he thought, disappointing Death with his questions and confused expressions, so he nods before Christopher can change his mind.

"Alright then," he says.

Once again Christopher prises open the doors and gestures at the darkness outside.

Noah hops voluntarily into the void.

☠

May 17th 2000

Noah is witnessing this memory as a ghost.

He's at the rehabilitation center in Manhattan where he successfully managed to conquer his Cocaine addiction. It had, by this point in Noah's life, already claimed his marriage and hospitalized him more than once.

Ogugbuaja Lauren appears in his peripheral vision. He's sitting on a wooden bench outside the glass doors at the front of the building and staring up at the unusually clear sky.

He thinks he can see stars.

Around the corner, armed with baseball bats and crowbars, are Noah Finn's drug dealers.

"Where is he? Where's Noah?" the leader asks; *demands*.

His face is covered with a black balaclava but Noah recognizes the voice. It's his dealer alright.

A dealer he was – technically still is - in major debt to.

"I don't know who you're talking about," Oggie lies.

Of course he does; Noah is one of their regulars and he'll be damned if he lets these rogues ruin his progress. In a few months Noah's sister Annaliese is getting married to a musician. Noah *has* to be there.

"I won't ask you again," says the dealer.

Oggie adopts an authoritative stance. He folds his arms, keeps his legs slightly apart and jerks his head to suggest they should leave. He even threatens to call the police.

The leader snaps his fingers.

The gang jumps him.

Oggie puts up a decent fight. He manages to prevent them from stepping foot through those doors, though one is accidentally smashed during the struggle, leaving a spider-shaped crack in the glass.

For once in his life his height and build are beneficial, but he soon tires and is overpowered. It isn't long before he collapses.

The group beat Oggie to death, leaving him for a doctor to find on his way to work.

"Mr. Finn's progress is too important," the

doctor tells the other volunteers when the ambulance drives away, "and Oggie wouldn't want to be the cause of a relapse. We'll re-locate Noah tomorrow. He need never know."

"What about the door?" asks the receptionist.

"Call in a repair guy. If Noah asks what happened, tell him it was vandalism."

Noah watches how calm and collected the doctor is as he arranges to deceive him, then phones the police.

His heartbeat hastens.

"*Oh God,* I remember him," Noah whispers.

"Oggie died for the greater good," Christopher says, tugging Noah away from the memory and back to reality, "and I already told you, there is no God."

September 11th 2001

"It hurts now, but Oggie was destined to save your life. That was his purpose; saved a few others on the way, too, but *you* were the primary reason he existed. That's why he was never married. He left no one behind."

"People still mourned him, though?"

"Oh of course! He fulfilled his duty, Mr. Finn. He got you to Annaliese's wedding. The universe, therefore, had no further use for him."

Christopher sits beside Noah and wraps an arm around his shoulder.

"Do you know that Ogugbuaja means *'innocence is stronger than sacrifice'*? From the moment he was born he was programmed to protect you. How does that make you feel?"

"Guilty! Terrible! Why was *I* so important?"

"Because *life* is important, Mr. Finn. Something you never understood, at least in relation to your own existence. Why else would you have swerved to avoid the dog that day?"

Noah inhales deeply. "A dog you claim saved my life."

"He died shortly after; death is to be expected when one fulfills their purpose."

"You're claiming a dog existed to get hit by a car, then stumble in my path so I'd swerve back onto the bridge. *Me - a* man who didn't want to be there anyway? It's a little hard to believe. If I'd have known about Oggie sooner, suicide would've been easy," he says.

"Good thing I'm only telling you now then."

"For animals to be involved in this 'save a life, take a life' cycle you're running, I'd expect more than, well, *you*, running it!" Noah scoffs.

"That's the asshole in your personality talking."

"Gee, thanks! I'm sorry-"

"All life is precious. Why has it taken you so

long to get that? Why did a plane have to hit a building and remove your choice once and for all for you to *see*? Why is this all so hard to believe?"

"Because life *isn't* always precious and you alone can't counsel every insect, plant and human life that leaves this planet," Noah argues. "There would have to be millions of you."

"Maybe there is. Don't let it bother you. You're dead and you're still in denial – concentrate on that. Shall I stop the train?"

Noah grumbles, "No, I've accepted my fate. I'm dead, I get it."

"I don't think you do."

"I didn't feel any guilt – I didn't feel *anything* - until you intervened with all your 'meaning of life' crap. Why is this only explained to us now? Why not at birth; whispered in our tiny ears to prepare us for how saving or taking a life will *hurt*? How can we all be responsible for one another?"

Christopher's eyes widen. "Whether directly or indirectly, we are *all* connected. Oggie died because you had to live. *You* died for a reason, too, but you're not ready to hear it. Right now, remember actions prompt reactions. And sometimes they involve people doing stupid stuff, leading to a loss of life. But, if they're lucky, they might *change* a life instead. A life like yours."

Noah pinches the bridge of his nose. "The doctor's decision not to tell me about Oggie's death changed my life for the better," he says. "I can't believe they were so protective of a man they barely knew."

"It was a rather noble act."

"Is the doctor still alive?"

Christopher smiles. "His time will come."

Deflated and hopelessly complacent, Noah slumps back in his silver seat and shrugs his shoulders.

He's done.

He's had enough.

Whatever lessons he must learn or personal flaws he must overcome to safely enter Heaven, they're far too complex for his simple human mind to comprehend, and he's too tired to fight.

No-one has ever quit or asked for a reverse journey before. Christopher won't let Noah Finn be the first.

Christopher offers a hand.

Noah takes it.

"Perhaps you do need to see Annaliese," Christopher asks, leading him back to the doors, "but you should brace yourself."

Chapter Nine
WHO KILLED ANNALIESE?

☠

October 6th 2000

Annaliese and her new husband Jose are being driven from the church to the wedding reception.

Her bouquet sits proudly in the back window. Noah sees she's now fingering the handkerchief and smiling.

Observing the incident from the front passenger seat is Christopher. Beside him is the driver; a stranger to their family, hired for the event. Occasionally he looks at the lovers in his rear-view mirror and scowls.

Noah is squashed between Jose and Annaliese. He ducks when the two lean in to kiss.

The car makes an unexpected left turn, throwing the occupants over in their seats and prompting Jose to yell at the driver.

They speed down an alley and pull up behind a restaurant where the driver gets out, drags Annaliese out by her hair, then screams at Jose.

From his belt the driver pulls a gun.

Panicking, Noah tries the car door.

It's locked.

"What are you doing? Let me out, I can help them!"

Christopher shakes his head as the violence unfolds outside.

"Thought you could rip off my music?" the driver yells, shaking the weapon and pacing behind Annaliese who is sobbing on the floor. "Thought you could ignore the law?"

Her beautiful wedding dress is filthy. Her knees and elbows are grazed. The driver is pulling her hair out at the roots as he yanks her around like a rag doll.

Jose denies knowing who the man is. Nevertheless, he begs Annaliese to forgive him.

Noah places both palms flat against the window.

His eyes fill with tears. He already knows what happens next.

This is a memory.

"You're gonna call your record label. You're gonna tell 'em who *really* wrote 'I Will Always Love Her' and you're gonna do it now!" A cell phone lands at Jose's feet. "CALL THEM!"

Jose stammers. "I, I c-can't!"

The driver rolls his eyes. Jose's response was as he expected.

So he squeezes the trigger.

Annaliese's head is thrown forward from the bullet's impact. A red mist sprays Jose's face and suit. The rest of her blood pools between them, crawling over the fallen handkerchief, staining it with hatred.

Jose roars and throws himself at the driver, using his black tie to strangle the man from behind.

Noah starts shouldering the window, attempting to break it, so Christopher unlocks the door.

He bursts out and lands in a heap, but he's too late.

The driver is no longer breathing.

Neither is Annaliese.

Jose kneels beside her body, gun in hand.

The noise must have alerted a local police unit because in the distance, sirens are wailing. If they catch him there, they'll think he did it.

"I'm sorry," he whispers, crying. "I'm so, so, sorry."

Noah's voice catches in his throat when Jose turns the gun on himself.

He pulls the trigger.

☠

September 11th 2001

An inconsolable Noah shoves Christopher away and sets off running through the carriages one by one, each identical to the last, until he reaches the end.

He pounds his fist against an emergency exit.

How could Jose betray Annaliese like that? Why didn't he protect her; save her?

Christopher appears behind Noah in the carriage.

He hates Jose. *Hates* him!

"Why did you show me that?" Noah cries.

"You knew your sister was murdered on her wedding day."

Noah nods.

"You knew her husband killed the attacker."

Noah nods again.

"Then why are you shocked?"

"Until now I thought he was a hero, committing suicide because he couldn't live without her. That's not true. He stole from that man, provoked him, then committed suicide in fear of taking the blame. It's his fault she's dead.

He's a coward and he should be in court facing the consequences."

"For stealing?"

"For murdering my little sister!"

Spittle flies from Noah's pursed lips and lands on Christopher's shirt.

He ignores it.

"You don't think suicide was ideal?"

"It's escapism," he says, pausing to think about his own attempted suicide. "I wanted to remember her for who she was, a beautiful, kind, caring and loyal friend to everyone. Why couldn't he love her enough to be honest? Why didn't he call his label?"

"Because there was no label," Christopher tells him.

"*What?*"

"Oh, not what you were expecting? Hmm, it's easy to blame someone – to point the finger unfairly – until we have the facts."

Noah wipes his eyes and slides down the door to perch on his bottom at the back of the carriage.

"Jose didn't steal any music," Christopher says. "He found the lyrics - a poem - on the Internet and thought it would make a beautiful serenade for his new wife, so he videoed himself playing and dedicated it to her."

"And the record label?"

"Social media." He sighs and helps Noah to a

stance. "Mr. Finn, when we first met I told you I'd been in a car accident. Do you remember?"

"Yes, hit by a cab."

"So you *were* listening. Good. It was in December 1999. Can you tell me who the perpetrator of Oggie's hit and run was that day?"

Noah scowls. "That homicidal driver?"

Christopher grins. "Now you're gettin' it. Oggie survived, but guilt is a powerful thing. It drove that driver to insanity. He was a fan of your brother-in-law's social media channel. It was their only connection. Something inside snapped; internal wires crossed."

"Did he even write the poem?"

"In his youth, yes, and Jose got a few messages about copyright but ignored them. He never tried to claim ownership. Annaliese loved the song and *she* told him not to respond. Innocent mistake, really, but one which ultimately led to their deaths."

"I *blamed* him-"

"He blamed himself. It's a lesson we must all learn someday, Mr. Finn, and for you, that day is today."

LESSON THREE
ANGER

E. Rachael Hardcastle

Chapter Ten
SUICIDES DON'T GO TO HEAVEN

☠

Noah is exhausted.

Christopher tries not to be amused. How can a dead guy, doing nothing but reflect on his life and sit in a train carriage, be *yawning*?

"I think you understand now," he says.

He mumbles, "How could I not? May as well have held that gun to *my* head."

"The perfect time for lesson three then." He smiles. "Anger and bitterness."

Christopher waits for Noah to say something sarcastic, roll his eyes or sigh.

Nothing.

"Not going to argue?"

"No," Noah snaps.

Beginning to feel an aching in his thighs and see the tender signs of bruising up his arms, Noah no longer wants to protest.

Death is claiming him.

In another four lessons he'll be gone forever.

At the end of the line, he imagines the rest of his body will reflect what he truly looks like. It's a frightening thought.

If he can endure whatever Christopher wants to show him, tell him, make him do, it shouldn't be long before he and Annaliese are reunited in Heaven.

And for her, he'd do anything.

They approach the carriage's emergency exit.

"I have a question," Noah says. "Back there you said if I committed suicide, I wouldn't be here."

"I did."

Noah scratches his chin, runs his hand through his hair. "So it's true? Suicides go to Hell."

"Why do you ask?"

"Because suicide's a sin," Noah says.

"According to invented ideals. There is no God to recognize such sins, though, no entity to punish them. Technically there is no Heaven or Hell, either, but you humans like to label things. I inspired it all, Mr. Finn. It's a work of fiction."

"If there's no Heaven or Hell, what happens at the end of this line?"

"You'll be given some interesting options. Suicides inconvenience me; they mess up my system and interfere with the order of the universe. I'm a busy man, so I show them how their selfishness affects others."

"Isn't that selfish of you, too?"

"Sure, but I'm Death so I can do what I like. You didn't commit suicide; this is all irrelevant."

"And Jose-"

"Went through the process."

"What were *his* options?"

"Concern yourself with your own future, Mr. Finn."

Noah perks up. "I have a future?"

Christopher waits, unmoving, by the exit. "Are you ready for your third lesson?"

Noah pauses. "What do you mean it's a work of fiction?"

"Religions weren't plucked from thin air. Before I was an observer, I planted the seed."

Noah raises an eyebrow and folds his arms.

"You're as guilty as anyone then. Is that why you're Death; you can't move on?"

"Actually, I like my job," Christopher replies.

"You didn't answer the question."

For the first time since Noah's arrival, Christopher's eyes glow red.

He gestures at the exit. "Last chance."

Chapter Eleven
INSPIRED BY THE DEVIL

☠

Noah Finn has, so far, learned the importance of and requirement for death. Specifically, sacrifice.

Oggie survived the hit and run to protect Noah at his rehabilitation center several months later, but also to allow the driver of Annaliese's wedding vehicle his murderous opportunity. If Oggie *had* been killed by the cab, the chain of events might be different.

Noah's head hurts thinking about who he could possibly have died for.

Christopher prises open the door and, using the backs of two seats as a brace, jumps up and kicks Noah into the void with both feet.

The thrust is incredible.

He feels his back snap, his legs buckle and his head crack. His neck is twisted. His lungs are chalky, burning. Despite the unusual sensations, there is no pain.

Just in case, he doesn't try to move.

"Comfy?" Christopher laughs.

Noah says nothing because his throat is so dry. His fingers twitch. If he could give Christopher the finger, he would.

"If I influenced mankind's view of God am I also partially their Devil? After what I just did I can't blame you for wondering. Of course that wasn't *really* me. It was your accident. A fall from a building that high takes its toll on a fragile body like yours, and I'm going easy on you."

Christopher's laugh echoes all around Noah until he slowly begins to regain movement in his limbs. Though he can't stand yet, he's able to lift his head and clear his chest of grit.

"WHAT THE HELL WAS THAT FOR?"

Noah coughs. Adrenaline begins to course through his veins again.

"Oh, *I'm sorry*. Let me help you up."

In the darkness Noah feels a hand touch his tender shoulder. He snags it away and, using language his mother would scold him for, warns Christopher not to do that again.

"No use being angry at *me*, Mr. Finn. I didn't cause such injuries, those terrorists did; religious beliefs did."

"Beliefs *you* introduced!"

"OK, clearly it's time we re-directed some of that anger. Now follow me."

☠

October 7th 2000

Noah feels a jolt; a tiny electrical shock as he's transported to another memory.

This time he's standing in a shiny white room that smells of bleach and other disgusting chemicals, where two technicians in laboratory coats are looking at a woman's body.

She is naked and stretched out on a long metal table. Beside her is a tray of instruments, some dripping red, and on a wooden hanger in the corner is a blood-stained dress and a clear plastic pouch filled with belongings.

Noah sees his handkerchief – the handkerchief he's stupidly lost - squashed at the bottom.

Discarded on the floor are Annaliese's shoes.

Noah covers his face and sinks to his knees.

"What's wrong?" Christopher asks.

"I can't see this. Take me back."

"You *can* see this and you should. What you'll learn is important."

"That's my sister. TAKE ME BACK!"

"I will not!"

Christopher grabs Noah by his collar when he

doesn't voluntarily move. He drags him kicking and crying to the table and holds his chin in position.

The scene is exactly as he imagined; disgusting, unnecessary and scarring.

"Why are you doing this to me?" Noah balls.

Christopher forces his head down to focus on some open paperwork, turning him away from the body.

"Because you were going to be an uncle, Mr. Finn, and I thought you worthy of such news."

Noah's eyes widen. He relaxes enough for Christopher to release him.

Because Noah can't physically handle the paperwork, Christopher gently blows to turn the page for him. He keeps a close eye on the technician in charge when it works, who scowls at an open window and continues working.

"I don't understand," Noah says.

"Your anger is blinding."

"Did she know?"

"Barely. Annaliese died when she did to save hundreds of innocent lives. The baby she was carrying would have grown to be an *evil* human being, through no fault of her own. A mass murderer, in fact."

"*My own kin?*" Noah gasps.

"Doesn't matter now. She did her job. She

prevented it."

"Did Jose know?"

"No."

"An entire family gone in one day? How could you take a pregnant woman and know for sure about the child's future? What about an abortion-"

"Oh, another sin?" Christopher shakes his head. "Parents do their best but in the end, children grow up to be whoever they are going to be."

Noah turns away. "I don't know what to say."

"How do you feel about her death *now*?"

"As I always have," he replies.

"Angry?"

"I was never angry at her."

"You're lying. You relied on her and she left you. For a while, you were angry."

"No, I was lonely and unhappy with the circumstances. I think she'd understand."

"She did." Christopher smiles. "She said you'd react this way; that I should shock you into realizing she died for the greater good or you'd be stuck on my train forever. She forgave you."

Noah offers half a smile and asks if he can return to the carriage.

Christopher tells him they have one more stop to make first.

Chapter Twelve
WHO CREATED THE CREATOR?

☠

Noah feels a blast of warm air.

Suddenly he and Christopher are kneeling at the front of St Paul's Chapel. There are flowers everywhere, intermingled with teddy bears, missing posters and mourners.

"Places of worship are calming. I feel at peace here, don't you?"

"I have a favorite place too," Noah tells Christopher. "The house where Annaliese and I grew up, where we lived with our parents. It had a big backyard where we'd play soccer."

"I'm pleased you have happy memories. You must miss your family."

Taking Christopher by surprise, Noah asks, "How can a man who laughs in the face of death be so interested in life?"

"Laughing in my own face? Never heard *that* before," he states, "but it's because death is not the end, Mr. Finn."

"Obviously I agree."

"Humans are *so* frightened of me; through the lingering fog of death they are unable to see birth, celebration, marriage, divorce, love, sacrifice and every other moment in their short, beautiful lives. Sacrifice is important, as is love. The two are usually connected."

Noah locks his hands in prayer. Although religion is useless to him now, having the one true entity beside him feels significant, like he owes it to those who still believe.

To those who are suffering in that plane crash right now.

To himself.

"If you're the entity we've been worshipping all this time, you must know-"

Christopher shakes his head. "I don't know the meaning of life or our purpose. I'm sorry. I, too, was created."

"But not by God. You were born, lived and died like me. Why did *you* get this job?"

Proudly, Christopher says, "Life was accidental. I was the first ever murderer, though, so naturally this responsibility fell to me."

"*Impossible*," Noah scoffs.

"Someone had to be the first, Mr. Finn."

"Animals were killing one another before we

existed. How about the dinosaurs!"

Christopher shrugs. "I said I was the first. I never said I was the first *human*."

"So what were you?"

"I don't remember."

"You're old, then."

"Yes, and we should respect our elders."

Without God, Noah can't comprehend how this entity exists. Who deemed him worthy of this job, why, and when? If he quit, how would humanity learn these lessons? Who would decide on Heaven or Hell for each soul; who would replace him?

And who's driving the damned train?

"Stop looking for answers to questions that do not - have never - existed, Mr. Finn. You'll give yourself a headache. If not by magic, how else can I exist in several forms at once, simultaneously helping those entering and leaving the world? I know everything there is to know about everyone. Conversations. Dreams. Thoughts. Actions."

"There's some other explanation," Noah says.

Magic is for bedtime stories and cartoons, he thinks.

Every question he has for this man has been formulated by his human mind to make the great void of incomprehensible information manageable.

The universe is far bigger than Noah or *any* of the people he ever knew, could grasp. Even those who assumed it revolved around them, like his boss.

"Tell me how religion came about," Noah says.

"No," Christopher says, standing. "It's time for your fourth lesson. Loneliness."

"I think I'm still angry and at *you*, if I'm being honest. Please, my wife Dylan is religious, so was my mother. Just answer the question, then I'll follow you anywhere."

"*Ex-wife*," Christopher says, making his way out.

"Alright, *definitely* still angry, *definitely* at you! For an omniscient overlord-"

"Be careful," Christopher warns, pausing as he reaches the doors at the back of the church.

"You can't kill me, I'm already dead. Put the train in reverse. Go ahead, I deserve Hell. As a kid I was a brat. I drove my parents crazy, almost to divorce. I ruined Dylan's life. Drugs. Alcohol. Gambling. Not to mention adultery. During my recovery I ruined Annaliese's life too, emotionally and financially." Noah offers his wrists. "Please, I *have* to know. All these flowers are in memory of people who deserved to live. They were good, honest people. If I knew why you created religion, maybe I'd feel less-"

"Less what?"

"I don't know, just *less*. Everything we know is a lie. If I'm going to Hell for asking then I'm not going to tell anyone else, am I? Why inspire us to worship - to *fear* - life after death?"

Quietly, Christopher replies, "You're just not ready yet."

holding out his picture. "I need to know he's alive."

Noah gasps. "She's looking for me!"

"She loves you, is worried about you. Always was. Always will be. Soon she'll be organizing your funeral."

"Our relationship ended badly. Why would she want such a tedious responsibility?" he asks.

Christopher scowls. The television screen goes black.

"Funerals are for the living."

"Nah, they're for the dead and are boring. They're dull and silent and upsetting for everyone."

"Funerals are necessary. They allow those left behind a means to process their grief - to learn these lessons but in their own way. Friends and family reconnect at funerals, share memories and find common ground."

"Hmm, well you must be right, being Death and all." His gaze meets his shoes. "Dylan met someone shortly after we separated, you know?"

"I can't understand why."

Noah ignores his attitude. "I don't know much about him except he's taller and broader than me, Hispanic, and he works somewhere near Central Park. He won't let her organize my funeral and I don't have anyone else. The state will cover it, I think. Still, he should be taking care of her so where is he?"

"Is that where you'd be, 'taking care of her'?" When he doesn't get a reply, Christopher continues. "Dylan's strong and independent, wealthier than you, she can manage."

"She has surviving relatives with cash, that's why."

"So did *you* until today," Christopher argues. "Did you not inherit Annaliese's finances?"

"Our parents' inheritance went to her but after the wedding payments, there wasn't much left. It was my uncle's decision. I got in trouble a lot, y'know?"

"Good thing, too. *You'd* have pissed it down the drain! Dylan will organize the funeral anyway; I've seen it."

Noah says softly. "She needs Lewis's support right now."

"We can still feel loneliness and depression even with family and friends close by, Mr. Finn. But, let's get back to why, and how, she's organizing the funeral-"

"Wait, you just said depression. Dylan isn't depressed."

"You say that with confidence."

"I am."

Christopher inhales sharply. "Mr. Finn, sometimes depression is so deeply rooted that its victims cannot identify it. How, then, can our family and friends? Dylan has been depressed for years. She even visited her doctor a few months before you separated."

Noah scowls. "She never said-"

"She assumed it was work-related stress," Christopher says, scratching his chin. "It wasn't. *You* fuelled her anxiety and fear. When you were home from work late - I use the word 'work' lightly, of course - she worried. Not about the possibility of another woman because she thought you were decent and loyal, but for your safety."

"I agree she was wrong about my morality but I was never in any danger."

"She worried about the busy New York roads, over-crowded subways, violent, anti-social youths in back alleys waiting to rob people. She thought about you often, prayed for you at night. That woman loved you, Mr. Finn, enough to make herself ill."

Noah sank back on the bench. Overall he'd been a terrible husband; more of a burden to Dylan during their marriage than a blessing.

"I've ruined more lives than I've enriched. She looks so *lonely*. I wish there was something I could do to show her I understand; to apologize."

Noah leans forward, covering his pale face with his hands. His shoulders tense. His toes and fingers scrunch up tight as he fights back raging floods of tears.

Christopher watches the display of emotion with a blank, detached expression. He's seen millions of reactions in his line of work, each unique and dependant upon individual morals and values. And Noah is no different, even in light of the tragic circumstances of both his life and sudden death.

The irony of it all upturns the corners of his mouth.

"Cry if you need to," he tells Noah.

"I'm not crying," he replies, sniffling. "I'm thinking."

"Pride means nothing here, nor does time, embarrassment or ridicule."

He gestures at the stationary train sitting alongside their platform then opens his mouth to suggest they continue.

Instead, after a thought, he says, "We're in no rush."

Noah begins to pace. "I've never felt loneliness like that."

"Like hers? Do you feel it now?"

"Terribly," Noah says. "I have nobody, nothing, nowhere of my own. Death has left me empty-handed; a beggar."

He frowns. "For what do you beg?"

"Prior to this I'd have said my life. *Now*," he says and lifts his head to the blank screen, "for

Dylan's. I want you to protect her."

"You know I can only observe-"

Noah groans and takes himself off into a dark corner. He slumps against a dirty grey pillar and slides down it, allowing his legs to sprawl out on the concrete platform. Dust and grit stain the back of his shirt and the rusty point of a bent nail rips a tiny hole in the hem.

"Humans take so much of their existence for granted. In death we are left only with memories and thoughts in, often enough, quiet contemplation. But death *is* the loneliest time, Mr. Finn, more so for us than those we leave behind."

"I think I see it, *feel* it, now."

"Which leads me back to your funeral-"

"I don't deserve one."

"That's not for you to decide."

"I've been a horrible person. Why would Dylan want to bury me when I ruined her life?"

"Don't flatter yourself, you were not the only cause of her pain. A human mind is a complex thing. The credit isn't *all* yours to take."

"But I cheated on her, used drugs in our apartment, got us in debt. The list is endless!"

"*No* list is endless. Not even for my clients."

He rolls his eyes and pats his top left pocket, where the list of the departed is safe.

"Can I see it?"

"No."

"Why not?"

"They call it *my* list for a reason."

"I can see who's next, though."

"And of what use is that information to you? You're dead, remember?"

"How could I forget?" Noah sighs. "I can redeem myself if I help you with your next client. Prove I'm not a complete monster. You and I could be partners - we'd *all* have someone with us at the end. Then I'd deserve a funeral."

"None of us are ever alone. Not really. That's what these lessons are for, Mr. Finn. You're afraid now but you're only at four of seven. There's plenty of time for you to *redeem* yourself, though really it's unnecessary."

Christopher snaps his fingers. The train door opens.

He steps inside.

"Like I said, there is no God, religion or sin to grant redemption. There is only me. Are you coming?"

Noah raises a brow. "Where to?"

"To lesson five, upwards."

Noah puts one foot on the train, feeling the sudden weight of his platform-bound foot. His body is telling him to remain at loneliness. It's easy to feel sorry for himself here. But he's not the only dead person and Christopher *did* say he'd be given options.

"Do not expect to defeat loneliness."

Noah's eyes widen. "You make it sound like a good thing."

"It helps my cause a little."

"Which is *what* exactly?"

"You'll see," Christopher replies. "Now come on, there's more to cover."

Chapter Fourteen
THE WORLD IS LONELY

☠

Noah sits in his original seat, contemplating his wasted life.

His knees judder. He nibbles the ends of his fingernails, staring at the black void through the carriage's reflective window, wondering what else Christopher wants him to learn about loneliness when already it feels like they're last remaining souls in the universe.

Thinking about Dylan's dust-covered face; her piercing blue eyes alight amongst the mass of terrified grey bodies surrounding her, Noah imagines she feels the same.

"Are they ever going to find my body? Is that why it's so easy for Dylan to arrange my funeral, because the coffin's..." he swallows hard, "...*empty*?"

Christopher grinds his teeth. "Depends."

"On?"

"Your options."

"I'm ready for them."

Christopher shakes his head and sits beside him.

Noah hands back his handkerchief, feeling cooler the closer to the seventh lesson they climb. He hopes this means he's heading in the right direction. To Heaven, or whatever sits in its place.

"Did I ever make it clear why you're learning these lessons?"

"No," Noah says. He folds his arms. "I think I understand anyway, though."

Christopher gestures for him to offer his version of the rules. Noah stands so he can pace. Physical freedom always made Noah feel comfortable expressing himself; capable of persuasion.

"My guess is that these aren't lessons but truths." He pauses and rubs his face, then sets off pacing. "You're showing me seven things about my life I never knew; seven important details I need to know to make a decision. The universe wants me to weigh them, know all the facts, so I'm not cheated when you finally reveal my options."

"What would I cheat you of?"

"A future, be it pleasant or a punishment. You can only observe; I, therefore, have to act, but you want it to be fair. Given the circumstances of my death, you want me to see how precious life is."

Christopher's mouth upturns. "Tell me, Mr. Finn, what have you learned so far?"

Without pausing Noah says, "I've accepted my death; what it means to die and the repercussions of suicide. You've taught me the order of things, human responsibility; that there's a reason for all life and death. You introduced me to Oggie, a do-gooder who gave his life for mine, even when it was undeserved."

Christopher smiles but says nothing as not to break his client's train of thought. He gestures for him to continue with a gentle nod of his head.

"You demonstrated the importance of actions and reactions and showed me how emotion is powerful when I blamed Jose for Annaliese's death. Emotion controls us, causes us to act foolishly but ultimately leads to forgiveness. It, too, is therefore useless in the end."

Noah inhales deeply, remembering their tragic deaths. He wishes he hadn't witnessed the cab driver's irreversible actions but no longer blames Christopher for forcing him to.

He'd bottled up blame and hurt. It was poisoning his soul, blinding him.

Listening, Christopher wrings his hands together and leans forward in his seat.

"But I'm still learning," Noah finishes.

All this, Noah knows, has so far demonstrated how one man's actions - *his* specifically - affected the people around them for better or worse.

He stops pacing, but remains standing.

"Earlier you said my loneliness helps your cause."

"It does. I have a proposition for you, Mr. Finn. One no man has *ever* received with their options before, but of course I can't tell you what it is yet."

"So what was it about my death that warranted this option? Why didn't you offer it to Annaliese or Jose?"

"Jose wasn't ideal and Annaliese would have said no or recommended I offer it to you. Anyway, the date, circumstances and irony of today represent *everything* I'm in the market for. My own past mistakes require corrections. To fix them I plan to use you, if you'll let me."

Noah cracks his knuckles. "By 'mistakes' you mean creating religion?"

Christopher shrugs. "What today has shown me, Mr. Finn, is that we must *never* meddle in affairs that are not ours to meddle in. I'm an observer now but that was not always the case. Even in death, we are only human."

"Except you're not really, are you? You tried to

influence mankind by creating a complex belief system," Noah says, "which is a pretty *epic* mistake. Are you going to tell me why you planted such an enormous seed?"

"My own anger clouded my judgment," Christopher explains. "Humanity holds no respect for the one true entity - you compartmentalize everything, break down my processes and label them. You are destructive, dishonorable, cruel and egotistical."

"As are you," Noah says.

Christopher doesn't argue.

"You are also liars, thieves, murderers and monsters beneath your fleshy exteriors. It is what it is, but you're unable to *own* or accept such a nature and instead you blame me. You curse me! You beg of me! You swear by me! I created religion to inject some worth and respect, kindness, love and hope into your lives and to give you something – *someone* - to blame. I wanted to prove myself wrong; show humans weren't just a destructive species.

"I spent so long teaching you the meaning of life, I forgot why I bothered in the first place. Through religion I hoped to control your actions; to make each of these post-death journeys easier for me and each of you. Instead you divided, started wars, argued, killed and continued to look to *me* for a way out; for the answers to questions you need never have asked."

"If not for you they wouldn't have."

"We'll never know, but herein lies my mistake. I injected religion to solve mankind's many woes and instead, I created chaos."

Noah moves slowly to his seat and perches on the edge, head in his hands, elbows on his knees.

There are so many questions he wants to ask Christopher Saint. If there is no God, was there really a Jesus and did he sacrifice himself for mankind? What relevance is Christmas, Easter, Eid, Hanukkah, Diwali and the other family-orientated festivals the religions of Earth annually celebrate?

Sensing his unease, Christopher clears his throat and snaps his fingers, turning on the flickering radar again so Noah can see how many clients he's dealing with as he deals with him.

Noah re-considers asking these questions because he already knows there will be a cryptic, awkward response. He'll only regret it and worsen his already *diabolical* headache.

There is, however, one burning question he does want to ask. As if reading his mind, Christopher stands and walks away.

"Yes," he tells Noah, "I'm the loneliest of them all."

LESSON FIVE
UPWARD TURN

Chapter Fifteen
OUR OWN WAY

☠

The train is once again in motion.

Noah stands this time, gripping a rusty metal bar for support. His head is down and his eyes are tear-filled; through his migraine he doesn't notice the man scurrying from carriage to carriage right away.

When Noah finally does see him, his stomach tenses. He still doesn't have his ticket.

The policeman's cheeks are flushed, his forehead is sweating profusely. He's screaming and shaking a flip phone in the air, but Noah can't hear any of the words.

Noah pats his pockets and begins to rummage, but with no luck turns to ask Christopher if the man's real this time or a harmless mirage as before.

Either way, Noah's got severe deja vu. He

knows that guy's face from somewhere.

But as Christopher is nowhere to be seen, Noah must quickly evaluate his options.

- Prise open the door and jump to his next lesson alone.
- Wait for the angry officer to reach him – hope they can work something out over his lost ticket.
- Run away to evade capture.

Before a confused Noah can decide, the officer is on him, begging that he take a step back. He holds out the phone and places it on the closest seat, almost in slow motion.

"More of us are waiting at the next station, Buddy," he says.

Noah is about to ask why when the door behind whips open. A gust from the tunnel drags him to the edge and he clings helplessly to it, eyes wide and afraid.

This doesn't feel like a lesson anymore.

It feels like a memory.

He blinks once.

Surrounding Noah is twenty-three concerned faces. Some are standing, others are sitting, and the policeman is planted firmly in the center. There's a woman shielding her son's eyes, an elderly couple frozen with fear and several businessmen and women on their way to work.

Not only did Noah take the train to work sometimes, he had also attempted to commit suicide on one of them.

He *remembers*.

"Hold on, Buddy, I'm coming to get you!"

His voice carries above the *tshuck tshuck* from the tunnel, the chatter and gasps of those in the carriage and, of course, Noah's own threats to throw his body onto the tracks.

Hearing a stranger pretend it's all a misunderstanding, calling him 'Buddy', makes Noah even more anxious. But still intent on taking his own life in front of innocent families, he grabs the phone and crushes it.

"No more police!" he orders.

Mortified by his own behavior, Noah steps away from his ghost.

He's not actually going to jump, the officer decides. *He'd have done it already.*

Strategically he shifts his attention to a little boy, shielding him from Noah's self-destructive behavior using hushed, calming words.

"It'll be alright," he tells the boy and his mother. "More policemen are coming. We're almost at the next station."

Jealous, Noah narrows his eyes. He turns suddenly and, with a brief running start, heads for the void. The officer drops everything and grabs Noah's wrist at the precise moment his first foot leaves the carriage's safety. With the assistance of two other businessmen, he pins Noah to the floor. Another passenger closes the door and a fourth pulls the emergency brake.

The train halts near 81st Street. Police and two eager paramedics jump on board, delaying the service for over an hour and inconveniencing hundreds of commuters.

Commuters who Noah once served and despised. Commuters to whom he now owes his life.

He blinks again.

He's back in his silver seat and perched opposite is Christopher Saint. He places a comforting, gentle hand on Noah's shoulder.

"I've tried so many times they're all just blurs," he says. "Why didn't he just shoot me?"

"Because he wanted to save your life, not take it," Christopher explains. "The human brain is an incredible machine. It blocks out painful memories for its own protection. You were traumatized."

"It was my second attempt, right after the rope snapped," Noah tells him. "I was determined."

"I know. I was there every time, *willing* it."

"Willing me to die?"

"Willing you to *live*."

"And the boy, was *he* traumatized?"

"You mean Tommy? No, he had nightmares for a while though."

Noah sighs and shakes his head. "I'm sorry."

"Don't be. Tommy wrote a report about it for school. Two weeks later when he heard the estimated suicide rate for that year, his class started a fundraiser. Together they spread awareness and raised money to support suicide survivors, backing rehabilitation and medication."

"That's wonderful, but it was still wrong to behave that way in front of a vulnerable, innocent kid," Noah says. "I'm ashamed."

Christopher starts to laugh. "If you have learned *anything* on this trip, Mr. Finn, surely it is that everything happens for a reason; is planned. The universe, despite trying to save you, knew you were a lost cause fairly early on. Because of this, something good could come from each of your attempts."

Noah is silent.

"At the age of twenty-two, that's in ten years, Tommy's best friend Michael will become indebted to one of the most *dangerous* drug dealers in New York City. You know him too; he killed Oggie. In rush hour traffic, after being missing for twenty-four hours, Michael will

throw himself off the Brooklyn Bridge."
Christopher pats his top pocket and winks. "He's
on my list."

"Why doesn't Tommy stop him?" Noah asks.

"We cannot *all* be saved, Mr. Finn, and
Michael isn't Tommy's responsibility. We are our
own people. We make our own way."

"Why are you telling me this if nothing can be
done?"

"Nothing needs to be done. Don't you get it?
Michael's death will fuel Tommy's motivation,
encourage him to campaign not only for suicide
survivors but drug addicts, alcoholics, prostitutes
- you name it. Processing his grief for Michael
opens Tommy's eyes to the world's evils. He'll
decide to fix them and at thirty, he'll be famous
for trying."

"After that?"

Christopher pauses, noticing the well of tears
in Noah's eyes as he waits to hear what he already
knows will be tragic news.

What else? After all, his business is death.

"According to one woman's extremist beliefs,
Tommy will be interfering with God's plan. She's
going to take a kitchen knife and attend one of his
conferences. When his security are on a shift
change-"

"STOP IT! I can't take this anymore!"

Christopher jumps. "You shouldn't ask

questions you don't want the answer to, Mr. Finn."

"It's not fair. Why can't *she* suffer instead?"

"Oh, she will."

"You said there's no Hell, so how will she be punished?"

"Life imprisonment," Christopher replies. "You humans are capable of solving your own problems. But, of course, there are her post-death options."

"I hope they're shit; that I get more than her!"

Christopher tries not to laugh. "Noted, taken under advisement. But yes, you'll have more; you were a nicer person and they're far more pleasant, but it's not a competition."

"You promise?"

"It means *that* much to you?"

Noah nods.

"OK, I promise."

"Are you lying?"

"Not that it matters, but no. A promise is a promise."

Despite Christopher's promises to divulge his options at the end of the line, Noah begins to question his intentions.

Why is it, he thinks, *we all receive options, even those who are not worthy? Who decides, if not Christopher, who is worthy? Am I worthy?*

Nobody's perfect – are we all docked an option for bad behavior? Could I have been a better Christian? If Christopher observes, he must know from birth what our options will be; what we qualify for and if not, who writes his list; sends him information?

If there is no God, who made him Death?

"I see you are beginning to question me again," Christopher says, interrupting Noah's thoughts. "I understand. Life, more so than death, is difficult for the young. You're still young, or at least you *were*. Human beings feel guilt more than any other emotion, intermingled with anxiety and fear. Can you believe that?"

Noah nods but says nothing.

"Humans are gifted with the ability to breathe air in and out of their lungs, to think, to listen to the THUD THUD of their own hearts, to communicate through artistic means, smile and play, laugh and feel the pulse of adrenaline coursing through their veins. More than anything else, though, you're all too busy with the affairs of others; with how your actions negatively impact or influence someone else. Why is that, I wonder?"

"Is that a rhetorical question?" Noah raises a brow. "Because that's something I *can* answer."

"That's why I brought it up."

Noah clears his throat. "I think we're always

worried about others, no matter how pleasant or successful our lives are, because of love," he says. "Love trumps all other emotions. It's strong and solid and everlasting."

"I disagree," says Christopher. "I think love is fragile, requires nurturing."

"I did too when my marriage failed," Noah tells him. "I still feel for Dylan, though. I miss her because I enjoyed her company. I will always love her and on some level, I *hope*, she'll love me. Relationships end. Memories, though, are far more permanent and personal." He taps his skull. "They're embedded. Escaping happy memories isn't easy. I hope those suffering as we speak are trying to think happy thoughts, remembering something cheerful and picturing the faces of their loved ones." He pauses and smiles. "*My* last thought was of Dylan."

"Not of Annaliese?"

"Strangely, no," he replies. "I guess I missed Dylan most; I knew Annaliese was in a better place and could take care of herself."

"Yet you're not a religious man."

Noah shrugs. "I was christened."

"You felt nothing of God at all?"

"Why would I? He doesn't exist."

But on some level he did feel a spiritual connection to someone, or something, he couldn't comprehend.

Perhaps, he thinks, *my love was for this entity? For life and death and all in between.*

"I think what I felt is programmed into all of us," Noah says. "I felt nothing of God as a man or a creator, but I felt plenty of joy, anguish, hope, betrayal-"

Christopher smiles and cuts him off.

Noah scowls. "Something funny?"

"No, I'm just pleased," Christopher says. "You're finally getting it."

LESSON SIX
RECONSTRUCTION

Chapter Sixteen
RECONSTRUCTION

☠

"I think it's time to revisit your death," Christopher says, extending a large, open hand to Noah. "Then we'll talk about your options."

For him to agree on the fifth lesson learned so soon, Noah must surely be making progress; developing on a physical and emotional level. He doesn't feel like it, but he doesn't argue, either, because he's another step closer to his options.

"I feel like such a disappointment. I assumed my options would be, well, *limited*."

"Everyone's options are limited, Mr. Finn. You're dead. There isn't much wriggle room."

They chuckle.

Noah notices Christopher's cheeks flush and his stomach tenses as he does so. It's a cute, sweet quality; one he imagines the real Oggie shared.

Christopher opens the door and steps aside, releasing Noah's hand to allow the jump.

Hopeful, Noah takes a jogging start and plummets into the void.

Suddenly it's hard to breathe. Ash fills Noah's lungs. It's humid and it burns, sticking to his throat like tar.

His ankles and wrists snap in unison, shooting vicious lightning bolts of pain up his limbs. An overpowering force kicks back his chin, wringing his neck like a wet towel.

His eyes and skin are itchy. He's partially deaf in one ear.

He's falling.

Falling.

Falling.

This is it, Noah thinks. *This is how I die.*

Through the clouds of debris he sees himself from behind, floating, following his dying body to the ground. The real Noah is still unconscious and plummeting.

Windows pass rapidly along with screams, searing flames and hundreds of escaping pieces of paper. The stench of burning plastic and furniture fills his nostrils, rousing the past Noah enough for his eyes to blink a few times, but nothing more. Soon enough the weight of reality knocks him out again.

Noah is actually pleased he wasn't awake for the next part.

Everything happens at once.

Noah's body clears the smog. He hits a roof hard enough to break his neck, but by this point his limbs are broken and deformed and his temple is pierced anyway.

Noah is pleased he died alone. It's unpleasant to say the least.

Christopher appears at his side, his hands interlocked behind his back. He's rocking on his heels although his feet are floating at least a meter above anything solid.

"Do you see it?" he asks.

Noah draws back to better evaluate the scene of his death. His arms, although jagged like broken twigs, are outstretched and flat to the surface and his legs are together and relatively straight, forming the shape of a cross.

"Hmm, I see it." Noah narrows his eyes. "A cross on the roof of Annaliese's church is no coincidence."

Christopher says nothing.

"I thought you had no influence? I thought I *fell*?"

"I don't and you did. This isn't my doing."

Noah stares helplessly at his lifeless form.

"You're going to take advantage of it, though."

Christopher shrugs. "It would be rude not to."

"You knew I'd fall like this; this is all

connected to my options. Why else would you show me?"

"Of course I knew. I see all. I am the past, present and future. I know who will die, how, when and where. I am the one *true* entity, an extension of the universe itself." He crouches beside Noah's body. "I was there the moment you were born, for every suicide attempt, and I'm here now, for your death. Everything I show you is linked to your options. That's why we're here."

Noah sits cross-legged near his corpse. Dust showers them, slowly hiding the religious shape from all who might prematurely see it.

Noah hopes the church will escape otherwise unscathed.

"Why are you only showing me now?"

"Everything in its proper order, Mr. Finn. The emergency services aren't going to find you for a while. In two days a helicopter will fly over here and spot your shoes."

Noah realizes his feet have snapped at the ankles, so the toes of his once smooth shoes now point backward, toward the sky.

Bile rises in his throat. He looks away.

"There'll be plenty of time to talk about your options. I know you're suspicious – even more so now - and are beginning to worry about my intentions."

"A little." Noah rolls his eyes. "What possible

good could come of a helicopter – I'm guessing a reputable news crew – finding and filming this tragedy? I mean, *look* at me!"

Christopher sighs. "It's a powerful religious symbol. Seeing a lost soul crushed by such devastating circumstances yet fallen in *this* position during those final moments, well, it'll bring hope and peace to so many."

"You're using my death to inspire people? So this is who I gave my life for – the families of my fellow dead?"

"That's right. Survivors, grieving relatives, people around the world hoping for peace," Christopher says. "A noble death. One you don't deserve. If I were you, I'd take it."

Noah shakes his head. "Ugh, at least the building is beautiful; I could have landed on a fast food restaurant!"

"Oh indeed," Christopher says, "St Paul's Chapel has a wonderful history. It survived the Great New York City Fire. It's the oldest surviving in Manhattan." He pauses, grins, then says, "Are you familiar with – do you *understand* – the word reconstruction?"

"It means 'rebuilding'," Noah answers. "Which I guess is what will happen to this poor church after today."

"Oh no. St Paul's will survive! I'm referring to the physical and emotional struggles of reconstruction. Rebuilding a life after death."

Christopher checks his watch.

It's 10:28 am.

Christopher snaps his fingers and suddenly he and Noah are standing by the roadside, watching Dylan grab helplessly at busy firemen and police officers.

New Yorkers fly by covered in filth and blood and Noah, for the first time since his death, begins to appreciate the scale of devastation.

The chapel's doors are open and the emergency services, amongst injured civilians, are running in and out to set up care facilities and first aid.

Suddenly, everyone stops.

Their dirty faces turn in unison as the north tower, less than 30 minutes after the south, collapses.

Dylan screams. She sprints away from the chapel where Noah now knows she'd be safe. He wants to grab her wrist and yank her back; guide her inside for sanctuary.

Christopher stops him.

Noah is about to learn what it means to reconstruct a life after death.

They follow Dylan for several blocks; walk when she walks, run when she runs. Noah even cries when she cries. Until, emerging from the sheet of grey ahead, is Dylan's new partner, Lewis, who is a muscular man with almond skin and brown eyes.

He's handsome. More so than Noah.

Between coughs, Lewis calls out.

"I can't find him, Lewis," she cries, taking deep but jagged breaths between each word. "He's dead. I know it!"

"Did they find his body?"

She shakes her head.

Noah is surprised. Her new boyfriend's response to the death of her old boyfriend is actually sincere.

"How are you here?" she asks, awe-struck.

Lewis points to a near-by news crew filming the scene. Coated from head to foot in the same mess covering everyone else in the vicinity, occasionally batting aside fluttering paper or ashes in the air, the reporter and her crew begin re-positioning their gear. A few blocks away is the chapel's octagonal tower. When first built back in 1766 it would have been the tallest building in the city.

It now sits in the background of their shot.

"Wait, you saw me on *TV*?"

"I couldn't believe it either but here you are. Someone up there is looking out for you."

Lewis drags her aside and holds her shaking shoulders, digging his thumbs tight to her collar bones to hold her full attention.

"This isn't happening, Lewis. He can't be dead."

"Either way we can't stay here. It's too dangerous. Think, if Noah didn't go to work where else might he be?"

A terrified woman and child pass them, followed by a businessman and a fireman shouting into a radio.

Dylan shakes her head. She can't think in this chaos.

Noah watches, eyes wide. He reaches out and places a hand on the back of her shoulder, merely inches from Lewis's fingers. He wills her to remember his normal route to work; the places he stopped for coffee, the stations he used.

Internally he pleads with Christopher to spare her pain, refresh her memory.

"*Dylan!*" Noah screams aloud. "*I'm here!*"

Her eyes widen as if hearing his voice, but the moment quickly passes.

"She heard me?"

"Not really, but emotion *is* powerful," Christopher says.

Dylan sniffs and smears her dirty face with tears as she wipes her eyes, then pulls herself together.

"He takes the subway." She nods, pleased with

herself. "Then Starbucks before heading to the office. Sometimes he meets Charlie, his friend from the other tower."

"Let's assume he set off to work as usual then. Can you remember the name of the station by his apartment?"

"116th Street," she says.

"OK. Let's go."

Christopher pulls Noah away and returns them to the train, dropping him uncomfortably in the silver seat.

"Wait, I want to see if-"

"If they find you? *Obviously* they're not going to. I already told you about the helicopter. Until then you're missing, presumed dead. Dylan already knows in her heart you're a lost cause; guilt and memories are fuelling that fire."

"And Lewis's fire? What's fuelling *that*?"

"Besides impressing the woman he loves?" Christopher jabs Noah's heart, pushing him back a little in his seat. "The kindness of his heart, maybe?"

Noah smirks. "Bullshit."

"Best not concern yourself *too much* with their relationship."

Noah scowls and folds his arms.

"Sulk all you want, but you're dead and can't do much about it. Dylan needs to move on, Mr.

Finn. It's all part of your lesson; part of what reconstructing a life after death means. It's the process of mourning; a process you've been going through yourself. Only difference is that Dylan has been mourning *you* much longer than you've actually been dead."

The train picks up speed and Noah notices he's swaying gently as it heads uphill. He's still on the right path – they're moving, and they're moving in the right direction.

Despite the hurtful things he's thinking about Dylan's new boyfriend, the circumstances of his death and the irritating riddles from Christopher Saint, the wise old entity still feels he's progressing.

"Can I ask you something?"

Christopher nods.

"Who *is* driving this train?"

Christopher stares at him.

They burst into laughter.

"*I am!*"

"So you're the driver, the teacher, the punisher *and* the fixer?"

That last title brings tension to Christopher's shoulders. Noah knows he's hit a nerve.

"I mean, with all your other responsibilities you're now attempting to fix something as huge as *religion*? There are so many. It's impossible; it must be."

"Nothing is impossible."

"*This* is. There's just no way you can counsel the thousands of dying people right now, drive this train, observe the world *and* initiate whatever fix you have planned for more than half the planet – a fix that involves me, right?"

"It's by no means a fix."

"Sure it is! You meddled. You created something you shouldn't have and you're trying to reverse it. Plus, you're hoping to use *me* and *my* circumstances to achieve it. Is that even legal where you come from?"

Christopher stands abruptly. "You wouldn't understand. Just know that everything is under control."

Noah says, honestly, "I may not have been a stand-up guy when I was alive, but I know anxiety when I see it. I've had my fair share and inflicted enough on others. My co-operation in this fix is important, isn't it? Am I just a means to an end?"

"I'm confident the road I'm *hoping* you choose is what you'll want for yourself, but ultimately the decision is yours."

Through his confidence, Noah smells Christopher's fear. Even after their earlier conversations about the relevance of human emotion, it's still there, solid as Noah's hatred of himself and his situation.

"You're not human. You never were," he says.

"I never claimed to be."

"You're trying to teach me the importance and risks of emotion but you have no first-hand experience! You don't remember what you were, yet you expect me to figure out who I am. Isn't that upsetting for you, not to know where you came from or who your family are?"

"Existing now is enough. I get to help people. People like you." He smiles. "Why is it important to you that I know all this?"

"You're showing me how to reconstruct a life after death. A *human* life. Besides observing and meddling in our affairs, you've never walked in our shoes. Your existence is here, in limbo."

"It's not-"

"Whatever you call it," Noah says, waving off his protest. "If I'm to meet your requirements, I should be honest, right?"

"Right. But I am *everything*, so there is no-one more qualified than I to teach you about life or death. You needn't worry. You're being tested fairly, I promise."

"Is such doubt part of reconstruction, too?"

Christopher nods. "Of course. Vital, even. You're entitled to ask questions; nothing stopping you moving back a stage, either. Time means

nothing here; we are free to put this train in reverse if you're still reluctant to move on."

"No, I just-"

"Just *what*, exactly?"

Noah sighs. "I feel like you're rushing me."

"Unintentionally, but I can see why you'd think that."

Noah exhales, relieved. "So, what's the hurry?"

Christopher scratches his chin. "This date has plagued me. I rarely ruminate, Mr. Finn, but I've been trying to avoid today's events. I wanted s badly to meddle again, but I couldn't."

Noah frowns. "You saw the planes hit before happened; why is it such a shock? If you were meddle, I'm sure it'd be allowed given circumstances."

"The temptation is intense," Christopher s "and though I expected these events, seeing cruelty is shocking nevertheless. I'm still tryi correct my first mistake, but no, nature mus its course. What is troublesome today will t another tomorrow. I stand by my teaching pauses, then asks, "What do you know Bible?"

Noah inhales deeply. "Very little. Neve but know of it. My grandmother kept a bound copy on her nightstand."

"And of Jesus?"

Noah nods. "Why do you ask?"

"To describe Jesus, what three words might you use?" Christopher asks.

Noah thinks. His lips twist in thought.

After a few minutes he says, "Sacrifice. Love. Hope."

"Ah," Christopher hums. "He certainly sacrificed a lot for mankind. He loved you – humanity, that is – too. You're absolutely right."

"Jesus was real, then?"

Christopher wrings his hands together. "Jesus preached for several years before he was crucified; a horrible way to die. But yes, he did walk this Earth."

"Plenty of people preach," Noah argues.

"Few die like he did, though."

"Did you counsel him, too?" Noah asks. "Are the stories true?"

"Some of them. Make up your own mind about the miracles he performed, the magic of his existence or how the Bible says your planet was created. Each religion has its own explanation."

"So which is correct?"

"None. All. Some." He smiles knowingly.

"I'm confused."

"So you should be! Mastering and understanding Earth's spiritual and religious workings are complex and a task not for the faint of heart." He says. "Do you know what your name means, Mr. Finn?" When Noah doesn't

reply, Christopher says, "Noah means 'rest' and 'comfort'. A fitting name for someone in your position, at least right now. Your final resting place, St Paul's Chapel, will be a place for recovery in the days to follow 9/11. Your surname, Finn, means 'fair'."

"I always thought I'd been named after Noah's Ark." He smiles, almost giggles. "I'm probably one of few who rather likes their name."

"It's endearing. How about your middle name?"

"I was never given one."

"Of course you were! It's written on your birth certificate – another pointless human tool to mark the introduction of a new life." Christopher rolls his eyes. "I wish I could show it to you."

"Me too. After my parents died Uncle Joe, then eventually Annaliese, took charge of their belongings, including finances and paperwork, keepsakes and such. I couldn't be trusted." He lowers his head. "When she died I put everything in storage."

"And to whom are your belongings willed?"

"To Dylan," he replies, "because I have no children."

"I see."

"Well," Noah says, eyes wide. "What *is* my middle name?"

"I was there when your mother chose the name

'Joshua'. Your father wasn't too pleased. He wanted something more masculine, like Clint."

Noah scrunches up his nose. "Joshua *is* a bit average, though I can't say I'm a fan of Clint, either!"

"The average names are often the most symbolic. Joshua means 'salvation'." He places a firm hand on Noah's shoulder and squeezes. "Did you know Joshua is a Greek translation of an Aramaic name? The original name was *Yeshu'a,* the real name of Jesus."

Noah shakes his head. "I don't understand what any of this has to do with reconstructing life after death?"

"Then it's time for you to learn about hope. The two go hand in hand. And so shall you and I to your final lesson."

LESSON SEVEN
HOPE

Chapter Seventeen
A DYING LIGHT

☠

"I'll be right back," Christopher promises. "I have to attend to something."

Then he's gone and Noah is alone.

He sits in his silver seat. His legs no longer judder anxiously, his palms and brow no longer sweat, his hands no longer shake.

He's accepted his fate.

He's dead.

And Dylan will never have closure.

The train slows and stops at 116th Street where Noah usually disembarks.

Wait, we're going backward now?

On the platform the television is playing the same tragic news story. The entire station is packed with people, all of whom look concerned, are crying, screaming, arguing or sat in stunned silence.

Noah stands and waves at a few of the faces, glaring helplessly in his direction, but they can't see him.

He hops off the train in time for the doors to close and quickly takes off a shoe to jam them open.

No one to yell at me now, Noah thinks.

But he's wrong.

A young man, similarly dressed to Noah and probably of the same profession, scowls at the jammed doors and hobbles over on his injured ankle to fix it.

Noah panics and sprints back to retrieve it, ensuring he's on the inside when the doors shut.

It's like something, or someone, is keeping him here.

When he turns to catch his breath, he is face-to-face with Dylan and Lewis. They're scouting the carriage, looking for signs that Noah was ever there.

Deflated, Dylan grabs the back of his metal seat when the train starts to move and glances up at the advertisements lining the walls. In one of the shiny plastic poster frames, she sees his face.

"Holy fuck!"

Lewis comes running. "What is it?"

Noah is frozen in shock.

"She can see me," he tells himself in a whisper, then louder and louder until he's convinced and waving. "SHE CAN SEE ME!"

Dylan touches the poster with the tips of her fingers, frightened if she acknowledges his presence he'll disappear.

"Lewis, is there anyone behind me?" she asks.

He scowls, shakes his head. "I don't-"

"IS THERE ANYONE BEHIND ME?"

"*No*," he says, jogging down the carriage. "What's going on? Did you find something?"

"You could say that."

"I'll call someone."

"I don't think they can help us now," Dylan says.

When Lewis is close enough, she points to Noah's reflection and waits, hopes and prays, he sees him too.

But he doesn't.

Noah steps forward, forcing Dylan to do the same. She may be pleased to see him but she's not quite ready to feel his touch.

Of course he's forgetting he's a ghost, but to Dylan he's vibrant and glowing; luminous like an angel.

"Can you hear me?"

Dylan shakes her head and taps her ears. She sees his lips moving but there's no sound. When she turns, there's nothing but a boring, grey train carriage and Lewis's large frame blocking her path.

She bats him aside, gliding through the puff of dust from his clothing as she makes her way down a row of silver seats, passing poster after poster.

They're all the same.

Noah follows her and smiles.

"I'm losing my mind," Dylan says. "What's happening to me?"

She breaks down in tears. Lewis consoles her with a tight embrace and leads her to the doors.

"I'm seeing ghosts!"

Noah knows he has to act fast.

With as much force as he can muster he grabs the frame with both hands and begins to rattle it, doing his utmost to tear it from the wall.

"It's OK, Dylan," he hears Lewis tell her. "It's part of the grieving process; it's normal. He's not really here."

"The *Hell* I'm not!"

Noah groans as he comes to the end of his strength. He sits, deflated, in the seat beside it and watches as Dylan wipes her eyes, preparing to leave the train and his life, forever.

Right on cue, Christopher Saint re-appears.

"And here I thought there was hope for you," he says.

Grinning and in one smooth motion, he flings the poster frame across the carriage, smashing it at their feet. Dylan screams but doesn't run. Through her tears she moves to the nearest poster to find him again.

"*Noah?*"

She laughs, cries a little, then laughs some more.

Lewis's eyes widen at the mention of her dead ex-husband's name.

"How are we going to explain this?" she asks without turning her head or waiting for Lewis's protest. "He's standing right beside me, trying to tell me something."

Lewis jams his foot in the door and prises it open again, then calls to a nearby policeman who is escorting a paramedic out to the street. He beckons them over, assuming the day's trauma has taken its toll on Dylan's sanity.

The paramedic attempts to sit her down.

Christopher rips down a second poster frame, then another and another until only theirs remains.

"Do you see him too?" Dylan asks the man.

Shaken and confused by the falling posters, the paramedic squints and tries his hardest to please her but ultimately shakes his head.

Noah panics.

I must get a message to her.

With the absence of a pen and paper, he can do nothing but mouth '*I'm OK*'. He holds his heart, so she knows he's sincere, and repeats the words over and over until she smiles and nods.

His light fades.

His reflection dims.

With tear-filled eyes she lets the paramedic lead her onto the platform and away from the train.

On her way out, she glances across at the bench where Noah once slept.

And there, covered in dirt and blood, is his navy handkerchief.

She's got what she needs now.

She doesn't look back.

Chapter Eighteen
OPTIONS, OPTIONS AND NOT A
MINUTE TO WASTE

☠

"You're welcome," Christopher says, drawing Noah's attention from the back of Dylan's head as she leaves, handkerchief in hand, to go home.

"I don't know what you did or how it was possible, but *thank you*."

He sighs and sits back in his seat.

"Again, you're welcome."

"Was that another lesson?"

"I called in a favor, but a lesson is what we'll call it." He winks.

"Whatever you did, I appreciate it." He smiles.

"I know, that's why I did it. I wanted to show you the light, Mr. Finn. It's brilliant and vibrant. Some see it right away; others, like you, take their time."

"So seeing the bright light in death isn't a figure of speech. People really do see something?"

"If their hearts actually stop beating." Christopher pauses, then explains, "Dylan has hope; she knows that for you - the man she loves - it's *not* the end. Now she can go on to fulfill her own destiny, save the life she's supposed to save, die for the person she's destined to die for. All without fear."

Noah sniffles. "You didn't have to do that. I'm your client, not Dylan. You broke the rules, for me?"

"I make my own rules," he says. "Now you both have what you need to move on. Hope is the most important stage; the most valuable lesson."

"Hope for what, though? The damage is already done – people are dead or dying out there. What use is hope to them now?"

"It keeps us marching forward. It's a beacon beyond all trauma, fear, sorrow. Hope is what prevents suicide."

"For what is *Dylan* hoping for, exactly?"

"A love like yours, as it was in the beginning," Christopher says, breaking off a fragment of Noah's heart. "Like everyone in the world right now, she's hoping New York can bounce back from this. That the terrorists will be caught. That those suffering – including you - will find peace. That she can move on to begin a new life with Lewis now she has closure."

"So *that's* why you helped us, so she could run

off with that buffoon?"

"Would you wish her to be alone forever?" When Noah doesn't reply, Christopher says, "You misunderstand. I did it to display the effects of hope on a human mind. There are 6,204,310,739 of them on Earth right now, and that number will only rise."

"What's your point?"

Christopher sighs. "I need you to help me inspire them, Mr. Finn. Are you ready to receive your options?"

Noah's mouth falls agape.

He's lost for words.

The moment he's been waiting for has finally arrived and he's utterly terrified.

What if the options aren't what he wants; what he deserves? What if they're *too* generous?

"It's that time already?"

Christopher snaps his fingers.

Noah is suddenly staring at the television screen. The platform is clear once again; they're completely alone.

"Yours was a difficult case," he begins.

The screen is black save for three white boxes reading one, two and three.

These are Noah's options.

Careful not to tempt an unconsidered decision, Christopher keeps hold of the remote control.

"It comes down to these," he says, then wraps an arm around Noah's shoulders.

He's trembling.

"Option One: Reincarnation. And before you do anything too rash, Mr. Finn, know you will *not* be human and it will *not* be in this time. We must avoid Dylan suddenly finding a blond-haired stray puppy now, mustn't we?"

Noah scrunches up his nose. "I'd settle for a kitten, you know."

"I think we've upset her enough."

Noah nods. "But I'm not a Buddhist."

Christopher tightens his grip. "There is no religion, Mr. Finn, remember? I can *still* put the train in reverse."

Noah holds up both hands in surrender. "Just sayin'."

"*I* influenced religion, Mr. Finn. Naturally some of their beliefs and rituals are based on truth. Others, not so much. I chose reincarnation for you as I believe you still have much to learn about this world; lessons better learned outside the human form. You may not live so many years, but you'll be back here for another round soon enough."

"Will I remember my time as a human?"

"No, I'll make certain of that."

"Then there's no point. I'll forget the lessons I'm learning here. I could end up with the same options." Noah raises an eyebrow.

"Choose reincarnation and you'll find this all out for yourself. I can't tell you any more. There are, of course, two others."

Noah raises a brow. "I'm listening..."

"Option Two: Extended Entity. I'll merge your soul with mine; fully under my control, you would reap the souls of the departed and, as an extension of my existence, do as I have done for you."

Noah gasps, "You mean I could do your job, like be a reaper; be *Death*?"

"In a way. How do you think I can be in so many places at once, understand so much, empathize with so many people, speak all these languages and exist outside of time and space? Together we'd prepare people for what happens next; identify their strengths and weaknesses and aptly recycle their souls."

"I'm up for that, I-"

"Wait for your third option, Mr. Finn, I beg of you. Solidify your decision too early and we can't go back. Patience *is* a virtue."

"Sorry," he mumbles, stifling his excitement, but still secretly eager to press the button for option two. "So what's the third option?"

"Reincarnation," Christopher says, straight-faced.

Noah scowls. "But you just-"

"This would be... different."

"*How* different?"

Christopher leads Noah to the bench. They sit side-by-side for a while, in silence.

"You know I've made many mistakes, Mr. Finn. I meddled. I created religion - I was foolish, uncensored and raring. Because of *me*, the intended injection of understanding and respect for who I am and what I'm capable of into the world got out of hand. My loyal followers split, then they split again and again until I could no longer keep track of humanity's beliefs, rituals and practices. Everyone focused on a different God, someone who could give them something newer and better than the last, particularly in death. Instead of acting, fearful I may make yet *another* mistake, I promised myself only to observe from that point forth; to let my error run its course. It seems I was once again mistaken."

"You've made lots of people happy through religion too," Noah says. "You should be proud of that."

"What people believed to be miracles were coincidences. What people asked for in prayer, confessed to in church, killed for in *my* name, all branched from one idea planted on one unfortunate occasion. This, I deeply regret."

Noah feels sorry for him. Clearly this has plagued him. Wanting to correct something and putting it off for so long in fear of making things worse, only to see mankind kill each other in such a way, must be difficult to bear.

"You're still capable of making those things a reality. You have the power to produce a miracle, to heal someone incurable, to answer a prayer, *right*?"

Christopher nods. He glares down at his empty palms, flexing his fingers occasionally.

"I can no longer use them; I've fallen weak, Mr. Finn. That's where *you* come in, at least it will if you choose Enlightenment."

"Hang on, you're offering to give me your powers? Like, *all* of them?"

"Yes. You will become their next savior. The world, especially after today, will need a leader. Someone who knows what it's like to die, to fear, to live in pain both emotionally and physically. They can no longer be trusted alone, to follow the path I laid for them. Incorrectly, it seems. They're out of control, polluting their own planet, *slaying* one another in my name. I am more than Death, Mr. Finn, but death, illness, cruelty, evil and pain are all they know right now. That has to change."

"And you think *I'm* your guy? I've been trying to kill myself now for the past, well, I can't recall how many years. I didn't respect or want my life; what makes you think I can make others?"

"Because you used the word 'didn't'." He

smiles. "September 11th 2001 will be a date remembered by all, not because of those who chose to do harm, but for those who chose to save lives in the name of community and peace, to give their time, their money and their skills to rebuild and regain what was lost. You can be a part of that, Mr. Finn."

"How, exactly, would I do this being dead and all?"

Christopher takes hold of Noah's hand.

"Now listen closely because this is going to get complicated."

Noah swallows hard.

"There's enough power left in me – power I trust – to make some changes. At the moment your body looks like Noah Joshua Finn but if you were to choose Enlightenment, you'd be given a new identity and everything you need to continue your life as someone new."

"So I wouldn't be me anymore?"

"The man you were is dead no matter which option you choose. *Yeshu'a* will replace you as the people's savior; if you'll help my cause, you can be resurrected."

"Dylan needs a body to bury," Noah says, pausing to chew his lip. "My friends and what little family I have left need to mourn. I couldn't deprive them. I *shouldn't-*"

"I'll take care of it. You'd be doing me a favor.

E. Rachael Hardcastle

The least I can do is pay it forward."

Noah shakes his head. "I can't believe you're offering to let me *live*. This is both tempting and disturbing. How can one man change the way an entire planet works, thinks, *feels*, though?"

"The way your religious leaders, politicians, celebrities and saints did, Mr. Finn. Inspire them, show them the way. There are no rules; tell them what you will. If you think they will benefit from knowing me and my role, share your experience, but be weary some may not believe what you say."

"I'll never have such an influence. I'll be locked in some institution for rambling nonsense."

"It'll be your job to make them believe. Convince them in any way you deem suitable. Write a book. Preach on street corners. Sing songs. I trust your judgment. You have known pain, suffering and disappointment just as this tragedy is forcing others to. They'll look for a solution, Mr. Finn. A man resurrected on 9/11, with a passion for kindness and a miracle to share can be that solution."

"People like that get assassinated."

"Until you select an option, I'm blind to your future. I can't tell you how this ends."

Noah shakes his head, through disbelief more than rejection, and begins to pace.

The temptation to live, to pass Dylan in the street again, to watch the news, learn to play the guitar, read more, laugh more, be grateful for his life, overwhelms him.

With such a gift there would be incredible responsibility too. Something Noah needs to address.

"And if I fail? What if I try to change the world and nothing happens? Will I be punished?"

"We can only try, and try again," Christopher replies. "And if we don't try-"

"We will never know," Noah finishes.

He sighs.

He owes it to himself, to Christopher and the people he's already hurt in life, to at least *try,* but is he the right man for the job? Can the mere shape of his fallen body do all this for him; inspire change while he helps Christopher to find the *real* savior?

"Alright," he says, "I've made my decision."

Christopher hands Noah the remote control. "When you're ready, come join me on the train. I'll get you where you need to be."

Christopher leaves the platform.

After a few more minutes of silent thought, Noah raises the control and selects his option.

He sets the control down on the bench.

He takes a deep breath.

He smiles.

Chapter Nineteen
TWO DAYS LATER

☠

September 13th 2001

It's 06:00 am.

Dylan is watching cartoons. In the kitchen behind her, Lewis is brewing coffee and preparing for a busy workday.

For him, it's business as usual.

For Dylan, it's day three of grieving in stage one of the process.

Despite seeing Noah's spirit on the train she's in denial. A world without Noah Finn – no matter his crimes or their past disagreements – is no world at all. Until the funeral in three days' time, her plan is to sit on the sofa and eat nothing but chocolate ice cream and cookies.

Afterwards, her plan will be to drink wine.

"I'll see you this evening," Lewis says, leaning

down to kiss her forehead.

Her eyes are red and swollen from crying, though they're currently dry. Her hair is matted; scrunched up in a messy bun and tied with an old scrunchie. She's wearing fluffy pajamas.

"Maybe try for a shower today, huh?"

Dylan scowls at the back of his head as he leaves to hail a cab. When she hears the door lock, she changes the channel.

On the news, they're filming the aftermath of Tuesday's tragedy. A helicopter is flying over the destruction and debris in the financial district.

What Dylan doesn't yet know is that 2,978 are dead, including Noah.

19 of them were terrorists.

2,754 died in New York.
184 died at the Pentagon.
40 died in Pennsylvania.

Dylan isn't sure how to feel or what to think. It's too early to register anything but pain.

Fighting tears, she reaches for her coffee.

In her peripheral vision, Dylan sees the crew are filming the church again. The reporter says it's a miracle there hasn't been more damage. Other than the expected dust and mess, all windows and doors are intact. They even zoom in on the roof which, although is covered in layers of debris, is in one piece.

The reporter pauses.

She urges the cameraman to pan left.

There, protruding from the debris, are Noah Finn's shoes.

Dylan drops her cup.

Chapter Twenty
THE STATION

☠

Startled by the sound of a passing train, Andrew Law awakens in a bustling subway station. He's stretched across an uncomfortable metal bench.

Disturbed by an unusual nightmare, Andrew misses the announcement and drowns out a panicked conversation between two policemen somewhere behind him.

He scrambles to his feet.

In the calm of a now empty carriage, dirty and damaged as a result of discarded litter and anti-social youths over the years, he sits in a silver seat.

The doors close. The train jolts forward.

It picks up speed and disappears into the eerie tunnel. Andrew squirms beneath the dim yellow lights of the carriage as they flicker and temporarily go out, leaving him with nothing but the sound of his own breathing.

It's tense, claustrophobic.

When the lights come back on he's not alone.

Noah Finn is a slender man, just over five foot five, with ghostly skin and light blue eyes; the complete opposite of Andrew Law who has mouse brown hair, khaki eyes and a footballer's physique.

They sit beside one another in silence, both staring at the ground.

Andrew is about to clear his throat and say 'excuse me' to go sit elsewhere when Noah Finn turns to him.

"What you in for?"

"Job interview," he grumbles. "Yourself?

Noah grins. "*Really?* Well, best of luck today, then. I'm not too keen on the subway myself; used to work night shifts down here. Disrespectful teens and grumpy businessmen." He pauses. "That's why I became a janitor."

Andrew sniffs, turns away and picks at the dirt under his nails.

"Name's Noah Finn," he says, offering a handshake.

Hesitant, Andrew lifts his head to acknowledge the greeting but ignores the outstretched palm.

Noah gestures at the beads of sweat lingering on Andrew's brow, most likely from his nightmare, then offers him a blue handkerchief.

"Don't worry, it's hot in here for most people at first," he says. "Now about that job interview..."

E. Rachael Hardcastle

DEDICATION &
ACKNOWLEDGEMENTS

♥

Noah Finn's story was difficult to write not only because of the tragic circumstances, but because at some point, in one way or another, I think we all struggle with life's challenges.

I wanted my readers to know it's OK not to be OK all the time – we're in this together; are connected, even if sometimes it doesn't feel that way.

For helping me achieve this, I'd like to thank the following:

♥ my family, for helping me to explore and thicken my vision for this book, but actually, **for everything**,

♥ my BETA readers, for ironing through the text and developing my research, despite their busy schedules,

♥ & my loyal readers, for buying and (hopefully) enjoying the book.

So if you're ever struggling, look to the sky. Think you can see stars?

You can. And the stars see you.

None of us are ever alone. Not really.

The facts & figures in this book are from the 911 Memorial & Museum website. For more information, please visit www.911memorial.org.

E. Rachael Hardcastle

ABOUT THE AUTHOR

♥

E. Rachael Hardcastle is multi-genre fiction author from West Yorkshire, England.

Rachael believes that through writing we face our darkest fears, explore infinite new worlds and realise our true purpose. She writes to entertain and share important morals and values with the world, but above all, she writes to be a significant part of something incredible.

Her novels face our planet's struggles because she believes that together we can build a stronger future for the human race.

www.erachaelhardcastle.com.

Lightning Source UK Ltd.
Milton Keynes UK
UKHW012009140921
390580UK00001B/165

9 781999 968816